THE NEW WINDMILL SERIES

General Editors: Anne and Ian Serraillier

207

A PAIR OF
JESUS-BOOTS

A PAIR OF JESUS-BOOTS

SYLVIA SHERRY

HEINEMANN EDUCATIONAL BOOKS
LONDON

Heinemann Educational Books Ltd
22 Bedford Square, London WC1B 3HH

LONDON   EDINBURGH   MELBOURNE   AUCKLAND
HONG KONG   SINGAPORE   KUALA LUMPUR   NEW DELHI
IBADAN   NAIROBI   JOHANNESBURG   KINGSTON
PORTSMOUTH (NH)   PORT OF SPAIN

ISBN 0 435 12207 X

For Kenneth and Mary Muir

Printed and bound in Great Britain by
William Clowes Limited, Beccles and London

CHAPTER

1

BILLY GRIFFITHS limped down the last flight of stairs, one hand clutching the bannister for support. In the harsh neon light, his face was screwed up with effort and anxiety. It was anxiety mostly, for Billy, crippled by polio when he was eight, was accustomed to putting a lot of effort into getting around.

His large tricycle was stowed in a corner of the entrance hall to St Catherine's Buildings. He unfastened the lock that secured it against thieves, climbed on, and pedalled along the hall towards the door, bumping familiarly over the one step at the entrance.

Then, with his head down, his brow furrowed, and his hair as usual on end, he went swiftly along the curved road that led to St Catherine's Square.

"Just a minute, lad!"

The deep voice came from well above him, as did the hand that suddenly arrested him by grasping the handle-bars. Billy didn't need to look up—and he didn't—to recognize Constable McMahon.

"Billy Griffiths, isn't it? And where're you off to this time of the night?"

Billy frowned concentratedly at his front wheel and muttered, "The chippy."

"Yer mam sent yer out?"

"Bingo."

"Is she, now? And where's yer dad?"

"Night-shift."

"So that leaves you and yer little brother alone, eh? Where's he?"

"Bed."

"He shouldn't be by himself. You hurry it up then, and get back to him. Not many people in Chan's chippy, so be back quick."

The handlebars were released and Billy pedalled off again, still frowning at his front wheel.

One side of St Catherine's Square had been pulled down several years ago to make way for St Catherine's Buildings, and now, in the shadows of the gateway that led from the Buildings into the Square, the gang waited for him, having witnessed his meeting with the constable,

"Billy's clatted on us!" hissed the Nabber, always suspicious. "He was talkin' ter the scuffer!"

"No, he didn't clat. He's not a clatter, Billy isn't," Rocky O'Rourke refuted vehemently. "He's a good skin. It was the scuffer stopped *him*. All right, is it, Billy?"

Billy nodded. He had been filled with nervous excitement to start with, and the encounter with Constable McMahon had left his mouth dry.

"Right then," said Rocky, "youse knows the set-up. The shop's in Joseph Terrace and we get in through the empty house at the end of the row. Mind youse remember there's still people in one house and we have to go through their loft, so keep quiet! Got it?"

The gang murmured that they understood.

"Come on, then—foller me and keep in the shadows!"

The gang went off in a silence that was most unusual for them, taking their way through the narrow dark streets towards Joseph Terrace. Rocky went first as usual, smallest of the gang except for little Chan, his shoulders hunched, his hands in his pockets. Rocky was the silent one, the only one who always wore sandals—Jesus-boots as he called them—because he hadn't any other shoes. Little Chan from the fish and chip shop followed eagerly behind him with Beady Martin alongside and the Nabber bringing up the rear, tall and gawky and always chewing something or other. Billy, on his tricycle, kept to the roadway beside them.

At the corner of Joseph Terrace they became even more cautious, for this was enemy territory. If the Cats gang were bosses in St Catherine's Square, Chick's Lot ruled over Joseph Terrace and the streets beyond, and were sworn enemies of the Cats. It was a daring plan of Rocky's, invading their territory.

But the Terrace was empty. Down one side loomed the other end of St Catherine's Buildings, lighted windows punched in a chequered design down its dark length, and opposite was a row of crumbling shops and houses, half of them empty, about to be pulled down. The Cats stopped at the end of the Terrace, huddling in the shadows of a partially demolished building.

"Right! Remember the plan. Billy keeps douse."

Rocky went like a shadow up an exposed staircase that still stood along one wall of the old houses. The others followed, and they disappeared through an opening at the top that led into the first house.

Billy sat on his tricycle in the shadows of the staircase, listening to the footsteps of passers-by on the road and the rush of traffic along Catherine Street. He clutched the handlebars of his bike and prayed no policeman and none of Chick's Lot came along and found him. If there was any danger, he had to give the cry of an owl three times. He was worried about this. His mouth was so dry and the others so deep in the houses beside him, they would surely never hear him. Besides, he'd never known of an owl hooting in this particularly crowded part of Liverpool.

Inside the abandoned house, the gang were moving cautiously through the darkness of the first floor.

"Yer know like, this floor's not very safe," objected the Nabber.

"It's all right. I've been over it," whispered Rocky. "Here, now—there's a trap-door in the ceiling takes us up into the loft. Give us a bunk up."

Rocky was bunked up, and fumbled wildly in the darkness until the trap-door yielded above his hands. He pushed it aside.

"Bunk us up higher!"

He got a grip and heaved himself into the musty chill and dankness of the loft.

Leaning down through the opening, he hissed, "All right. Come on, Beady."

They scrambled up, one after another, until only the Nabber was left below.

"What about me? I can't reach!" he complained, and made one or two jumps in an effort to reach the trap-door.

"Shurrup!" warned Rocky. "There's people next door. They'll hear all that bloomin' racket!"

"Well, what about *me*?"

"There's a box in the corner ... Don't *drag* it about, but. Lift it!"

With the help of the box, and being taller than the others, the Nabber was able to heave himself into the loft without being bunked.

They stood in a bunch in the darkness, and then Rocky switched on his torch. It had been his brother Joey's torch and was now Rocky's proudest possession.

"There's no windows up here so we can have a bit of light. But no noise, mind youse!"

"I also have torch." Little Chan switched on one that

4

rivalled Rocky's in power.

"Put it off! It's like Blackpool illuminations! One's enough, wack. Now, see this door—it leads into the next loft. When we get through that we'll be over the shop. Take your shoes off though, and walk quiet. There's people underneath next door, see."

Rocky, silent in his sandals, didn't remove them, but the others obeyed his instructions. Rocky pushed open the small door and stepped through quietly.

He shone his torch for the others to follow, then showed them the small space, congested with water tanks, that they had to cross. The boards squeaked under their feet and they held their breath with apprehension. At the other side was another door, and they got through safely.

"Glad that's over!" Rocky wiped his face with a grimy hand. "That was the rough bit. Now we get into the shop."

"How do you know there's nobody there?" asked Beady.

" 'Cos I made sure, that's why. It's been empty a week, but I reckon they'll have left some stuff there still. Come on."

The Nabber was lowered first from the loft since, being tallest, he had less distance to drop and should have made less noise. But the bump seemed to shake the building, and the boys crouched petrified with fear waiting for someone to come and investigate. Nothing happened.

"It's all right," breathed Rocky. "Go on then, Chan."

Eventually they were assembled on the empty first floor of the shop, and Rocky used his torch cautiously in search of pickings.

There was nothing there. Wallpaper hung from the walls in great strips; there were holes in the floorboards and a black gap where the fireplace had been; in a corner, a heap of rubbish, including two odd shoes; on one wall, an old picture. That was all.

"Whose idea was this, then?" asked the Nabber scornfully. "Big deal this was going to be—and the whole place is empty!"

"The stuff'll be downstairs," insisted Rocky, though with slightly less confidence. "Anyway, I bet Chick's Lot never done nothing like this."

In the shadow of the staircase, Billy was getting cold. There were rats scuffling in the rubbish and a noise of shouting had started up somewhere further along the street. Billy wondered whether he should warn the gang. Cautiously he pedalled out to the street. At the corner, where the light from the off-licence was bright, was a group of youths he recognized as Chick's Lot, fooling about.

What was he to do? Chick's Lot would have to be passed on the way back. At the far end, a white mini police car was stationed and he could hear the crackling voice of its radio. Billy gulped nervously. What was it? A police raid on Chick's Lot, or had they been tipped off about the Cats' break-in?

In a panic he gave what was intended to be the hooting of an owl, and pedalled off desperately in the direction of Chick's Lot.

As he passed them, he heard one say,

"Hi—that's one of the Kittens, isn't it? Let's get him."

"Naw—better leave it—the scuffers are along there …"

It was Chick's voice.

Billy reached St Catherine's Buildings safely, and breathlessly locked up his tricycle. He limped upstairs and let himself into his home. His mother wasn't back, and his brother was still sleeping. Billy helped himself to a couple of biscuits and went to bed.

6

CHAPTER

2

"WHAT d'yer get last night?" Billy asked as the gang gathered next morning.

"A big load o' nothin'," said the Nabber scornfully. "Might have known—doin' an empty shop! Who lined that up, eh?"

"Well, there might have been something. And if you think yer can do better, you try it, mate!" Rocky rumpled his hair angrily. What did they want to go and lock up a shop for like that if there was nothing in it? he wondered. When it was empty and going to be pulled down anyway? Just to waste people's time! He scowled at the Nabber with a look of extreme disgust. "Whew! Yer don't half go off *some* people!"

"All right! I'll line it up next time."

"You try it. I'd like to see what happens."

"Well, you will."

"I'll bet!"

They were standing outside the newsagent's shop in Larkspur Lane, the small row of shops that lay at the bottom of the Steps leading out of the south end of St Catherine's Square. They met there every school-day, and put off the moment for going to school by gazing into the shop windows. There was Pa Richardson's grocery with special offers in the window and an advertisement for Brooke Bond tea. Next to that was Chan's chippy which always smelt of frying fat and vinegar even when the door

7

was closed. Then there was the small mysterious shop that never seemed to be open with a dirty window full of sun-faded blankets and children's clothes. And then there was the snack bar, grimy and generally deserted, though you could buy iced lollies there.

But it was the first shop, the newspaper shop where Rocky collected his weekly comic, that was most interesting with its collection of advertisements printed on post-cards. The boys stood there, gazing in at the jumbled paper-backed books, old comics, cheap balls and toys, a packet of balloons from last Christmas, notebooks and ball-point pens, and "Join Our Xmas Club" in the middle.

"Hi, have yer read that— *The Masked Rider*? That's smashing. It's all about this feller ..." began Beady, pointing to a comic book with a lurid cover.

"I've read that—it's nothing, that's not. Yer should read *Spider Man* ..."

"My father batter me," little Chan put in.

"What for?"

"Because I am late."

"Yer should sneak in the back," advised the Nabber.

"Back door always locked. I must go through shop."

"Why's it always locked? I'll bet yer dad's got a lot a money in there, hasn't he?" asked the Nabber, with growing enthusiasm.

Little Chan became suddenly cautious.

"No, we are very poor people. My father works hard, but he has to send money to our relatives at home."

"In Hong Kong?" asked Rocky.

"No, in China."

"You got relatives in China, then?"

"My grandfather and my eldest aunt still in China. Very poor."

"There was a break-in at the Buildings last night,"

8

said Billy.

"Go on!"

"There was. Two flats was done. I don't know what they took. It was the other side to us—the Terrace side."

Rocky's eyes narrowed with excitement. That meant there were two break-ins last night. While the Cats gang were doing the shop in Joseph Terrace, somebody else had gone into St Catherine's Buildings. So, although they hadn't known it, the Cats were practically working alongside some real crooks!

"Well, we didn't see nothing, did we?" he commented. "Come on. It's getting late." He huddled into his inadequate clothing as if to keep out the cold by a gesture and led the way along Larkspur Lane. "Come on, tatty-'ead!" he called over his shoulder, and his step-sister Suzie who had been standing listening, her nose red-tipped with the cold and the remains of a slice of bread and margarine in her hand, trotted after him.

The Cats walked in silence, pondering the news of this real break-in at the Buildings, until the Nabber concluded, "Well, I'll set up the next one!"

But the appearance of a policeman at the school that morning in conference with the headmaster changed their minds.

"What's up? D'you think they're on to us?" the Nabber asked. "Bit much if they cop us for a job we didn't make nothing on!"

Rocky was silent. Suddenly he realized what it might mean if the police *were* on to them. After all, they'd done nothing but get into an abandoned shop. It had just been a bit of excitement, really—something to make you sweat. But maybe that wouldn't make any difference.

Rocky rubbed an uneasy hand through his red hair and his tiger-yellow eyes stared into the distance as he saw himself trying to explain that to a policeman.

Suddenly he made a decision.

"We'd better lay low."

"What'd'yer mean? Lay low?"

"Saturday—better make it footy, and forget the lorry-skipping for a bit. Have we got alibis for last night?"

"You was all with me playing cards at our place while me mam was out," said Billy, frowning, and blinking through his glasses solemnly.

"Right. Mornin' break, Billy, we'll see the Chick's Lot and arrange for Saturday. Pass the word."

Billy was secretary and manager for the Cats football team, and Chick's team were their main rivals. No other team they'd played at Princes Park had ever beaten the Cats team except for Chick's Lot, and they were all slightly older than the Cats.

This season, Rocky was determined the Cats wouldn't be beaten.

Billy passed the word, and at morning break Rocky and Billy, Chick and Spadge ... Chick's second ... cautiously approached each other in the centre of the school playground —about the only neutral ground on which the two gangs could meet without a battle.

There was something peculiar about Chick and Spadge that day. Rocky and Billy felt it straight away. They were swaggering more than usual and they seemed to have a lot of private jokes that kept them grinning. It irritated Rocky.

"How's the big gang leader then?" asked Chick. "Hear yer did a job last night."

"Who said?"

"Police fairly turned the place upside down last night, didn't they, Spadge? The questions they asked us! I told them. I said, 'It's not us yer want, mate, it's them terrors the Cats Gang!'"

Chick and Spadge submerged in mirth, but Rocky said nothing. He felt cold all over. Surely their unsuccessful escapade couldn't have caused that much upheaval? Surely the police couldn't suspect them of the St Catherine's Buildings break-in?

Billy licked his lips dryly and took out his notebook. Billy took notes of everything.

"That wasn't us did the break-in—youse knows that. We want to arrange a match. Saturday morning. All right?"

"All right. If yer want to be beaten." Chick and Spadge laughed again. "That all?"

"That's all."

The two pairs of boys separated and turned their backs on each other and retired to their own areas of playground.

"Let the team know, Billy," said Rocky, "Practice tomorrow night."

"What about tonight?"

"I'm going ter the youth club."

"Think we'll beat them, Rocky?" asked Billy.

Rocky didn't answer. But his tiger-yellow eyes were determined.

"Practice in the yard at the Buildings," he said.

"Yer know we can't play there. It'll cause trouble … "

"Who's going to stop us? There's no caretaker just now."

The caretaker of St Catherine's Buildings had left a week previously, and no one had arrived to take his place. Some of the tenants might object to the boys kicking a ball round in the courtyard, but there would be no one official to chase them off.

It had been a wet afternoon but, by the time Rocky got

back to the Square after school, the clouds had ceased to drift in from the Mersey, the rain had stopped, and a bright, white patch of sky over the river cast a pallid light across the town.

Outside number 3 St Catherine's Square stood the old pram, as usual, containing Ellen-from-upstairs's baby, which was always there, hail, rain or snow. Rocky gave the pram a friendly rock as he passed into the hall.

Number 3 was regarded by the rest of the Square as the most disreputable house, and the families living there were regarded as the roughest and least desirable. Certainly they were the poorest, and the house was the dirtiest. But Rocky never noticed these things. Hungry and glad to get out of the cold, he stepped into the narrow hall with its permanently musty smell of damp and dirt, and its ragged linoleum. Rocky's family lived in the two ground-floor rooms, and he rushed straight into the front room which served them as a living-room where he knew he would find his mother beside the small electric fire.

"Hi, Mam, can I have sixpence?"

"What d'yer want sixpence for?"

"For the youth club."

"What d'yer want sixpence for them for?"

"Well, there's subs is threepence and a cup of tea."

Rocky waited anxiously, his red hair ruffled, his brow furrowed. He didn't get any regular pocket-money and apart from what he could pick up outside he had to ask for every penny he wanted. And he simply had to go to the youth club.

"Well yer can't have it. Yer can't go out there tonight, not unless yer take Suzie with yer."

"But I can't, Mam! She's too little for it. She couldn't get in!"

"They couldn't keep her waiting outside for yer if yer

took her," said Mrs Flanagan cunningly. "Anyway, yer can please yerself. I'm going to the bingo and yer'll have to watch Suzie."

Rocky stood looking out of the window, kicking his foot angrily against the skirting board. He couldn't take Suzie to the club—he would look daft. So he would have to miss. And he needed to go. Rocky didn't think much of youth clubs. He didn't like being organized and chivvied about. He didn't like reading in the quiet room, or playing snakes and ladders, or soppy treasure hunts, or doing exercises. He didn't even think much of the cup of tea and a biscuit. But he attended at the Baptist hall every week he possibly could from September to December. After that he never went back again until the following September. His interest ended in the youth club's Christmas party, which was the object of the exercise.

"Well, so yer staying in, are yer? Now no bringing that lot of hooligans in while I'm out tonight, and just run down to Pa Richardson's for some messages. I'll give yer the money ... "

His mother took out her purse which, for once, seemed to Rocky's eyes crammed with notes.

"Hi, Mam! Where'd yer get all the loll?"

"That's for me fare down to see Joey next Tuesday, so you keep yer greedy eyes off it. Pawned me best coat to get that, I did."

"Will our Joey be out soon?"

"He will, luv. Thank God! Poor soul. Fancy them putting away a young lad like that!"

Rocky's first hero was his elder brother Joey—'our kid' as Rocky always called him. Joey was in prison for stealing but only because, as he told Rocky, he'd been framed. It was only treachery could put a clever fellow like Joey in clink.

Joey had always been his mother's favourite, the pride of the family. He was good-looking and well-mannered and always had a joke. As soon as he could, he had a motor-bike and a black leather jerkin with studs all over it. He wasn't just leader of a kid's gang, like the Chick. Joey went on his own, and he made friends with some big-time men. Joey used to tell Rocky stories about how he put one over on this fellow and that one, but mainly on Jim Simpson, who was in the one-armed bandit racket.

Jim Simpson was rich—he had night-clubs as well, and he came from London and knew the set-up, but he couldn't put anything over on Joey. Rocky had once seen him come after Joey, and he never forgot it. It had been in Lodge Lane, where Joey had gone to buy something for his bike at a garage, and Rocky was with him. As they came out of the garage, a Jaguar pulled up beside them and a bald man with a moustache leaned out and shouted some abuse at Joey, something about doing him this time.

Joey had just laughed. He'd left Rocky and gone running along the street, and the Jaguar had followed him, but Joey was cunning and dashed across the busy narrow street and ran back towards Rocky. The Jag couldn't turn straight away, and Joey had stood jeering at the man in it, then he'd skipped off down a narrow alley.

Rocky never forgot that, even though, soon afterwards, Joey was arrested and sent to prison. It was all through Jim Simpson, as Rocky knew. Rocky's favourite dream was getting his own back on Jim Simpson, because he'd framed Joey.

When Joey comes out, Rocky thought, gazing out into the empty Square, we'll get Jim Simpson—the two of us together, we'll go after him.

His mother's voice cut into his thoughts, suddenly

harsh and scolding again. "Now I'll be away all next Tuesday, so mind yer look after Suzie, and the two of yer go to school."

Rocky did not reply. Plans for Tuesday began to form in his mind. He could scat school and have a whole day to himself—maybe go down to New Brighton on the ferry. But he'd need money to do that ...

"D'yer hear what I'm sayin'? Yer'll look after our Suzie and go to school ... "

I could maybe get some money off Pa Richardson when I go for the messages, Rocky thought, oblivious. A sudden slap across his ears brought him to.

"D'yer hear me?" yelled his mother.

"Ow! What d'yer do that for? I didn't do nothing! What yer always picking on me for?"

"Get yerself off for them messages ... "

Still protesting and muttering under his breath, Rocky left the house. For a second he hesitated on the steps, scowling across the Square as he worked out his plan for getting some money out of Pa Richardson.

Even on the brightest of days, walking across St Catherine's Square was like crossing the floor of a deep shaft. On three sides the Victorian houses with their sooty fronts stretching from submerged basements to dizzy attics and on the fourth side the huge block of flats all blocked the light and left only a square of sky high above the pavements. On a darkening September evening like this, the square took on an air of mystery very quickly, its corners and doorways smudged into black caverns and scattered lights going on in a motley collection of rooms and flats.

And above the houses at the bottom of the Square rose the red tower of the Anglican cathedral, brightened by the rays of a sun that had long since deserted the Square, with a misty hint of the river and the docks below and beyond showing through a gap in the houses.

The view seldom troubled Rocky. He had lived all his life in the shadow of giant buildings and he rarely noticed them. The streets were *his* world—and he knew those in his own territory very well.

For him, going out into the Square meant a moment's indecision as to which path he should take across it. In the centre of the Square was the hillocky plot of clay that had been a garden many years ago and now had an abandoned car in one corner and a builder's hut in another. He could cross that, or he could run along the parapet of the wall that surrounded it to get the Steps at the bottom of the Square. Or he could go left and take a right turn as he did when calling on Beady.

If he did this, he would pass the corner where there was a strange house—different from the rest. It had two gates, one leading between high walls up a narrow, tangled path to the back, the other leading into a walled garden at the front. The gang used to hunt for spiders in the cracks of the old damp wall. A solitary old woman lived there and was never seen except when she suddenly darted out at some passer-by, shouted unintelligibly at him, and darted back again. She used to frighten Suzie, but Rocky just used to shout back at her.

He chose the wall this time, slippery with rain. Tucking his hands into his sleeves to warm them, a pound note clutched in one hand, the old basket swinging from his arm, he set off. Rocky preferred walking on a wall to a pavement any day. His father used to say of him that he would never walk on a road if there was a roof handy.

As he ran, the wind, which always seemed to be blowing about the Square, whipped round his legs, whirling rubbish into corners and dust into his eyes. And a sheet of newspaper suddenly rose up and chased him for several yards, like a dishevelled and desperate cabbage.

He leapt off the wall in the far corner where the small, black church of St Catherine's stood with its crumbling vicarage beside it, both abandoned now, and ran down the Steps to Larkspur Lane.

CHAPTER
3

PA RICHARDSON'S shop was small and stuffy, smelling of paraffin from the heater and bread and potatoes and cheese. And Pa Richardson bumbled about behind the counter like an underfed bee.

"What's yer bacon?"

"Four and four a pound. How much d'ye want?"

"Will yer cut it thin 'cos it costs too much to cut thick."

Pa Richardson sniffed as he moved over to the bacon slicer.

"They know it all these days, Mrs Wilson," he remarked to another customer.

"They do that. Too much, some of them."

"Have they caught the lads that broke into the Buildings?"

"Not that I've heard of."

"I could—sniff—put the police on to something, if I wanted."

Pa Richardson had a habitual sniff, and regarded Rocky and the Cats with suspicion always. He didn't trust any of them and, moreover, he had a disconcerting habit in conversation of hinting that he knew a lot more than he was saying, if he chose to tell.

"Could yer now, Mr Richardson?"

"Ay—sniff. I can always tell. They—sniff—start spending more."

Mrs Wilson nodded sagely. "I know who yer mean. I've

seen them lately—putting more bets on. That lot from Joseph Terrace."

"Least said," sniffed Pa Richardson. "I don't want any broken windows."

Rocky listened avidly. So it was Chick's Lot did the Buildings. No wonder they were so cocky. And that meant they were in it for real. They weren't just playing about. Rocky gritted his teeth with annoyance. They'd think nothing of the Cats now.

"How's that brother of yours?—sniff—when's he due out?"

"Don't know. Soon now."

"That'll be more trouble."

"Our kid's a ... "

"I know all about your kid, don't you worry. But I'm not talking, yer can tell him. Now what else?"

"Gimme a big tin of beans ... and a cut loaf ... and a packet of crisps—cheese 'n' onion ... and them three cakes ... the pink ones ... "

"Who's the man with the grey Jag?"

Rocky looked up at Pa Richardson, startled but cautious.

"What man with a grey Jag?"

"I don't know—sniff—who he is. Came in yesterday—sniff—for cigarettes. He got chatting and said he knew your kid—sniff. Asked if he was out yet ... That all?"

This was a shock to Rocky—Jim Simpson, checking up on Joey. Asking when Joey would be back so's he could get him. Somehow he had to warn Joey.

"That's six and eight ... sniff ... one pound note ... and here's yer ... sniff ... change ... that's ... "

"Thanks," Rocky began to turn away quickly, the change clutched in his hand. If he could get out of the shop, he could return in a few minutes and say he'd got the wrong change—he could make a couple of bob that way.

But Pa Richardson was up to it.

"Just hold yer horses ... Let's see that change, lad. Mrs Wilson," turning to the customer, " ... sniff ... yer won't mind checking this, will yer? ... sniff ... six and eight out of a pound that's ... sniff ... thirteen and four. And that's what he's got, isn't it? Right, Rocky. I've got you!"

Rocky scowled and turned away, "He must of come over on a razor boat, he's that sharp," he muttered.

The gang had gathered in the Square, wondering what to do with themselves since Rocky was going to the youth club. Seeing him, their hopes rose.

"Hi, Rocky! Yer not goin' to the club?"

"Yer comin' out, Rocky?"

"I'm comin'. We'll go an' play footy. Can yer get the rest of the team?"

"It's too late now," said Beady. "Nearly dark. They won't come." The Cats co-opted several other boys in the Square to make up the Cats football team.

"All right. *We'll* go. We'll play in the yard at the Buildings."

"There's a new caretaker there now," said Billy.

"Uh?"

"He's a wingy—got one arm. Old feller."

"He couldn't stop us playing, I'll bet."

"Moved all his stuff in yesterday. He had a lot of pictures—footballers, they were."

"Our Joey had footballers' pictures all over the bedroom wall. Me mam took them down when he went and put them away. Said Suzie might spoil them. They're on top of the cupboard. I could get them and put them up in the hideout. Joey wouldn't mind."

"Ah, come on, Rocky, if yer coming," said the Nabber.

"Wait till I put these messages in ... "

His mother, as usual, sat reading by the fire. Rocky got the football. He hesitated at the living-room door.

"Hi, Mam, are yer really going' to see Joey on Tuesday?"

"I said so, didn't I?"

"Well, can yer give him a letter from me?"

"A letter from yer? What d'yer want to send him a letter for? I can tell him anything yer want. Save all that trouble."

"But I wanted ter … "

"Anyhow, they wouldn't let me give a letter to him."

"Oh well. It doesn't matter."

No good telling his mother about Jimmy Simpson—she'd only create. Better wait till Joey got out, then, first thing, he'd warn him.

Outside, the baby in its pram was roaring so loudly it could be heard as far as Pier Head. Rocky did a little cautious probing.

"Hi, Ellen!" Rocky yelled at last, up to the window above.

A window ground open and Ellen's head appeared, the long hair falling about her face.

"What's it?"

"He's in a right mess here!"

"Oh lord!"

Ellen's head was withdrawn and Rocky shot off to join the gang.

Beady pulled out of his pocket a large roll of sticking plaster, somewhat fluffy from the lining of his pocket.

"Hi, look what I've got!"

"Hi, that's smashing. Let's have a bit. Here look— we'll be the White Band gang!" cried Rocky. On his instructions, they got some scissors and each boy decorated himself with a large strip of plaster, on the right leg. Thus arrayed, they marched off shouting noisily,

"We're the White Band gang,
Come and catch us if you can!"

And, still shouting, they entered the courtyard of St Catherine's Buildings. It was a noisier, rougher game than usual, the restlessness coming from Rocky and spreading to the others. The caretaker didn't appear and Rocky began to lose interest. But at last, he did come into the courtyard. He stood, in a corner by the door to his flat, saying nothing, but swaying slightly on his legs.

It got Rocky down, that watching.

"You keeping douse on us, mate?" he asked at last, cheeky as he could.

"All right, boys, all right," said the wingy, not very clearly. "That's a fine game yer playing! It takes me back, it does."

Rocky was nonplussed. He'd expected the man to chase them.

"Up the team, eh! Liverpool for ever!" shouted the wingy.

The boys drew closer.

"Yer a team, are yer?"

"We're the White Band team," said Rocky, and everybody sniggered at this because it wasn't their name, after all, but the wingy wouldn't know.

"Who'd yer follow? Everton or Liverpool?"

"The Pool!"

"That's right, lads!"

As they got nearer the wingy, the reason for his strange behaviour became clear in a certain aroma round him. He was tipsy.

"Hi, he's a lush!" said Rocky, digging his elbow into the Nabber. "He's drunk!" And to the wingy, "Hi, mister, yer going ter chase us? We're not supposed to be playing here."

"My lad," said the wingy, "if we all did what we're supposed to, we'd be machines not people. Let's have the ball. Come on—come on—get it off me!"

And to their amazement, he grabbed the ball and went off with it, dribbling it up and down and across the court-yard with great skill, even if he wasn't sober, and the gang went haring after him. They got the ball at last, and the wingy stood panting.

"I can't do it like I used ter," he explained, "it's the breath, yer know—it's gone. Always remember the breath, lads. That's the thing."

"Hi, mister, yer norra a bad player," said Rocky, torn between admiration and derision.

"Not a bad … ! Here, I'll have youse know I once played for Liverpool!"

"Gerrup!" they shouted, derisively. "Yer codding, aren't yer?"

"Codding?" he regarded them with swaying seriousness. "I'm not codding. I used ter play for the Pool."

"Will you lot keep quiet there! Clear out!" a voice shouted from a window above.

The wingy put his finger to his lips. "Ssh. Youse'll lose me me job. Here, come on in a minute. The wife's out. If youse wouldn't mind taking yer boots off at the door … "

Fascinated by this unusual invitation, the Cats dropped off their shoes and entered the minute living-room, cram-ming themselves into corners and breathing heavily down each other's backs as they strained to look around them.

Everything in the room was neat, clean and tidy. Not a thing out of place, not a finger-mark anywhere.

"This is me … " Proudly the wingy drew their attention to the photographs of himself with the Liverpool team.

23

"Don't touch anything, for God's sake, or yer'll have the wife on to me. Breaks her heart if she finds a speck of dirt. You ask yer dads if they remember Davey Oliver. Oliver— don't forget ... See, I had to give it up. Lost me arm in an accident. I had to stop." He looked sober and sad for a few minutes, then brightened up.

"Never mind! Liverpool for ever! Oh! God save our gracious team!" He began to roar the Liverpool supporters' song, and, hilariously, the boys joined in at the tops of their voices. As the noise died away, angry protests came from outside.

"What's all the noise?"

"Yer can never get a bit of peace here."

"Where's the caretaker?"

"Youse'll lose me me job," whispered the wingy. "Get out of here the lot on youse ... " And outside, he stood swaying on the doorstep, fumbling in his pockets. "Just a minute ... " He pulled out a handful of loose change and promptly dropped half of it. The boys scattered to pick it up.

"Oops," said the wingy.

"Hi, now, you give Mr Oliver his money back," Rocky ordered, honest since he saw they'd get it anyway. "Hi, Nabber, give him that tanner back! Here ye are Mr Oliver. It's all there. Yer can trust us. But yer can't trust many round here."

"Right, then. Hold yer hands out. There yer are ... and there yer are ... Buy yeself a motor car with that ... " He doled out coppers into the expectant palms and Rocky, suddenly taking to him, confessed,

"You know like, mister, we're not really the White Band gang. We was only codding yer with that. We're the Cats, really."

"The Cats? Oh, aye. I've heard of your lot. Lot of

24

terrors, you are, aren't yer?"

"Who said that? We're not! They only say that …" Rocky protested.

"All right, son. I believe yer. Thousands wouldn't. Give a dog a bad name …" And with a final shout of "The Pool for ever!" the wingy retired.

The team scattered through the now dark archway and into the lamp-lit streets.

"Hi, he's a nut!" shouted Beady.

"He's a lush! How much d'yer get? How much we got altogether?"

Being in sufficient funds, they dashed off to Chan's for chips with plenty of salt and vinegar, and then sat on the Steps eating them, finishing up by licking the greasy papers.

Rocky's thoughts returned to his immediate problems.

"I'll bet he'll help us, the wingy. I'll bet we beat Chick's lot this season."

"I'll bet …"

Their voices faded through the Square as they went home, the crumpled chip papers left lurking in the shadows of the Steps.

Rocky and the Nabber were the last to go home. The others all had some kind of parental rule to obey in getting in at a certain time. But Rocky and Suzie were never remembered until they were wanted for an errand or until they turned up, and the Nabber seemed to have unlimited freedom.

They stood round the lighted window of the newsagent's and Rocky and the Nabber talked about the breakins that had made this gang or that gang famous. The excitement and mystery of the streets at night, when everyone who passed seemed to have an added and strange significance, the darkness of the churchyard beyond them, and the looming height of the cathedral above them—

Rocky loved this.

"Tell yer what, Nabber, before our kid comes home, I'm doing a real job."

"What?"

"Don't know yet, but I'm thinking about it. Will yer come in with me?"

"I'll see," said the Nabber. "If it's a good job, I might ... "

CHAPTER

4

ROCKY was wakened on Saturday morning by screams and cries. Sleepily he turned over and through the open door to the living-room saw Suzie crouching on the bed and crying while his mother shouted at her. Rocky sat up.

"Aw, shurrup, Suzie! What's the matter?"

"And yer'll stay in bed till I *say* yer can get up," shouted Mrs Flanagan. "She's tore one of my books, that's what's she's done, and she's been told to leave them alone. And you get out of bed."

Rocky groaned to himself. "She's at it again," he thought, while his mother's voice went on scolding and Suzie's cries rose.

Rocky spread margarine on some bread for Suzie, and she sat on the bed with it, her sobs gradually dying. He grabbed some himself, seized his football, and escaped from the house. At ten o'clock, the Cats gang with seven more boys from the Square alighted from the bus on Princes Boulevard, scattered across the road, and with a long whoop erupted through the gates of Princes Park, down the stony path, and on to the stretch of rough ground. Rocky was in front, the ball under his arm, the red of his shirt where it showed through the holes in his jumper clashing horribly with his hair. Red was the Cats' colour and it was displayed in various shades from pink to purple in the team's shirts. One or two boys sported football boots, but most of them had only ordinary shoes.

The September morning was bright, with a sharpness in the air. A scurry of light rain hit the team as they raced across to mark out a pitch, but it passed quickly and the sun shone again.

"Right, lads, pile yer coats at this end—this is our goal. Where's Chick's Lot? They're goin' ter be late."

Chick's Lot arrived and stripped off black leather jerkins to make up another goal. Billy tossed and Chick's Lot won, choosing to have the Cats playing into the sun.

"All right, Kittens," grinned Chick, "let's have yer."

The group gathered.

"What yer betting?" asked Chick. They generally had a bet on the result of the match, and the winning side got the money.

"We've got three bob from the whip round," said Rocky, with some satisfaction.

"Three bob? Here, we'll put down a quid. Maybe that'll encourage youse," said Chick, waving the note under Rocky's nose.

Rocky glared at him. "Yer a big-'ead, Chick," he snarled. "And I bet I know where yet got that!"

"Do yer now? Where?"

"From the Buildings. It was your lot did the Buildings."

"Miaow! Miaow!" mimicked Chick's Lot, and ran to take up their positions. The match that day was fierce.

Rocky arranged his team. Beady was always in goal—he was a good goalie, and Rocky played centre-forward. The Nabber was always right half because of his size and speed. Little Chan made a fair wing forward, because he was quick and skilful with his feet. And the rest of the team wasn't bad. Billy stood on the side-line, carefully watching the game, so that he could give his advice about future tactics to Rocky.

The Cats started off ferociously. The only advice Rocky

had given them was to beat Chick's Lot into the ground, and this they tried to do. But although it took them near the other goal once or twice, the ball was taken from them each time and was soon past Beady and into the goal.

It was no good. They tired soon because they used their energy quicker, they hadn't the skill at dribbling and passing that Chick's Lot had, and somehow or other Chick's Lot worked as a team—they always knew who was ready for the ball.

Rocky was in a flaming temper, what with the goals mounting up, and Chick and Spadge's grinning comments about the Kittens being too young to be away from their mother.

When Billy called time, Rocky stalked off without a word to get his coat, leaving Billy to hand the winnings over to Chick's Lot, and made for another exit to the park. He had no desire to get the same bus as that lot.

The rest of the Cats team dispersed, but the gang itself followed Rocky somewhat disconsolately, stopping to throw some stones at the geese on the lake for the pleasure of making them hiss. The lake glittered in the sun, the trees around were just beginning to show autumn tints against a pale blue sky, seabirds swooped white around and fought over scraps of bread, the skyline of big houses formed a circle all round. It was a day to be happy in—but not for Rocky. His feelings of hurt pride burnt as red as his hair.

"We'll beat Chick's Lot yet," he muttered. Sometimes Rocky got into moods like this, when he felt he was burning up inside with anger at everything, and couldn't do anything about it. Then his red hair seemed to be redder and his eyes yellower.

Whatever he did was wrong—his mother complained,

his teachers complained, the coppers complained. So he'd let them—and give them something more to think about. When his father had been alive, he'd been able to help. Things had never been as bad then. But now his father was dead and Rocky objected to his stepfather. Not that he had anything really against him, except that he had no right there, taking his father's place.

Rocky, thinking of his accumulated objections to life, rubbed his hand through his hair and hunched his shoulders.

"We'll beat the daylights out of them," he growled.

The Cats re-entered the Square with an air of defeat. They loitered a few moments, kicking the ball about, before separating to go to their homes.

"What yer doing this afternoon, then?" Rocky asked, hoping to fill in the barren stretch of day before him.

"I have to go out with me mam this afternoon," said Beady.

"Where to?"

"Me Auntie May's for tea."

"Huh! I wouldn't go out with me mam anywhere," retorted Rocky scornfully. "That's sissy!" And he wouldn't, in fact, even walk down the street with her if he could help it—not now that he was thirteen.

"Might see yer around," said Billy.

"My dad's taking me to the match at Everton," said the Nabber.

The gang dispersed and Rocky was left in the settling gloom of a Saturday afternoon with nothing to do. Smells of frying surrounded him from windows and doorways, a transistor blared pop music, two dogs fought in the far corner and a group of kids was skipping on the waste ground. Rocky noticed that Suzie wasn't with them.

Then, something his father used to say came back to him.

"Yer never know what to expect in this life, Rocky. Today yer wih the pools; tomorrow yer run over by the Pier Head bus. That's life. So you enjoy it as it comes." It hadn't meant much to Rocky at the time, except that he was for a while worried in case he ever won the pools and consequently got knocked down by the Pier Head bus in Princes Boulevard. But now he thought perhaps he understood. Things weren't so good for him at present, and maybe they'd get worse. But maybe they'd get better. Take it as it comes.

And when Rocky entered the passageway of number 3, he saw that the door of their kitchen was open and he heard a man's voice. Rocky stopped dead as he saw a policeman come out into the passage followed by his mother who was still in the old coat she used as a dressing-gown, her pale, plump face framed by her extraordinary black hair in curlers.

"Now, Mrs Flanagan, we're only making inquiries."

Rocky screwed up his face. He hated to hear his mother called Mrs Flanagan. Mrs Flanagan! It always embarrassed him at school and places when he had to explain that his mother was not Mrs O'Rourke—not any longer. "She's married again, mister." There was only Joey and him O'Rourkes now.

"What's it all about? What are yer pestering my boy for again? Yer did the same with our Joey. Never let him alone. And there's others get off scot free. I could tell yer about some of them ... "

Rocky made a quick movement, hoping to escape, but they heard him and turned to him.

"Ah, this is Rocky, is it?"

The policeman looked down at him, seeming to take him all in in detail.

"Rocky O'Rourke of number 3 St Catherine's Square.

31

And Tuesday night, Rocky, yer were in Joseph Terrace, that right?"

Rocky looked up at him sharply, his eyes narrowing.

"No I wasn't—honest, I wasn't," he exclaimed, beginning to protest innocence immediately.

"At about eleven p.m. ... Come on now, Rocky. No point in denying it. One of our fellows spoke to yer—asked yer what yer were doing out so late and got yer name and address. That's why I'm here ... "

Rocky guessed straight away it wasn't him they were after—it mustn't be the shop break-in the policeman was here about after all. With the relief he felt, his fighting spirit took charge again.

From an assumed indignation, Rocky swept into an actual one. Him? In Joseph Terrace at eleven? Him spoken to by a scuffer?

"Hi, mister, yer codding! It wasn't me! I never spoke to no scuffer!" His face twisted into a grimace of suspicion. "What yer all up to? Trying ter pin the Buildings job on me, aren't yer? Trying to frame me like our Joey was framed?" Rocky leapt into a defensive position along the passage, ready for flight. "Yer not taking me in, copper—yer'll have to catch me first!"

This outburst startled the policeman and Mrs Flanagan. The policeman was nonplussed for a moment, and then grinned, for something about Rocky protested a true innocence and Rocky's assumption that he was worth framing was comic. But Mrs Flanagan saw it differently. She had been ready to defend Rocky at first, but such talk of names and addresses being taken and Rocky's own outburst, confused and terrified her.

"Yer'd better know straight off," she said. "That boy's getting out of hand. It's a worry to me. I can't do nothing with him." Her voice rose suddenly in a shout. "Nothing

32

with him! He's out of control! He'll have ter be taken away! Just like our Joey ... !"

Rocky groaned. "She's off again!"

The constable looked from one to the other.

"Now, Mrs Flanagan, I think the best thing will be for you to come down to the station—Rocky and you—and let's get it sorted out ... "

It took some arranging to get Rocky and Mrs Flanagan ready and off, but eventually they followed the policeman to the station, Mrs Flanagan with a scarf over her curlers and Rocky still protesting his innocence.

Ellen-from-upstairs wearing her mini-skirt and with a scarf over her head came halfway down stairs.

"Eh, Mrs Flanagan, whatever's the matter?"

But Rocky's mother was too full of emotion to explain anything. She flapped a weak hand and choked. "If Suzie comes in for her dinner ... "

"Don't worry. I'll see to her ... "

In the Square, women came to their doors to watch.

"Yer see what's happening there?"

"Well, there's one in that family went that way already, and when one goes, the rest generally follow ... "

It only confirmed the opinion of the Square that Rocky O'Rourke was a bad lot.

Up to that time, Rocky had only known the police station from the outside as a rather quaint, squat building in red brick with lots of narrow windows, where, if he were in a daring mood, he shouted objectionable remarks and ran off fast. He'd never been inside before and he went in now belligerently, and was rather surprised to find a dusty, down-trodden interior. The desk sergeant looked over the closed half of a split door into the narrow passage where the party was assembled. It was like the infants' school gone to the dogs, Rocky thought.

33

The desk sergeant looked down on Rocky's fiercely upturned face.

"So this is Joey's brother," he remarked. It infuriated Rocky.

"Yes, mister, and just you wait. Our Joey'll be out soon and when I tell 'im how yer tried ter frame me, he'll be along to see yer—you bet!"

"He should be taken away! I can do nothing with him! He's like this all the time," put in Mrs Flanagan.

"She's off again!"

"Now then. Now then. Let's get it sorted out. Wilkinson about?" the sergeant asked the constable who had brought them in.

"Just coming, Sarge," and another policeman appeared. "Yes, sir."

"Have a look at this youngster, Wilkinson. Know him?" Wilkinson shook his head. "Don't recall him ... "

"He's Rocky O'Rourke. Yer took his name and address in Joseph Terrace the other night."

"Well then, there must be two Rocky O'Rourkes—because that's not the one I saw ... "

"Two Rockys! I hope not!" murmured the sergeant, and Rocky burst out, "I told yer—I told yer they was framing me, but yer wouldn't believe it ... Framing me, like they framed Joey!"

"Looks like it, Rocky. Somebody gave your name and address instead of his own. Now who would that be? Somebody who knows you."

Ideas whirled through Rocky's head. It was Jim Simpson framed him! The crook! The same fellow that framed Joey and got him put in jail. He was getting Rocky out of the way before Joey came out, so that Rocky wouldn't be able to help his brother. It was a big plot ... And then, quite suddenly, it clicked. Chick's Lot. That was their

34

territory. There'd been a break-in, and Chick's Lot did it ... One of them tried to frame Rocky.

The sergeant saw the change of expression on his face, and asked, "Well, Rocky? Any ideas? Somebody tried to frame you. Somebody who didn't want us to have his own name and address. And that suggests somebody who had something to conceal, don't it?"

Rocky closed his lips tightly, scowling. Not as easy as that, scuffer, he thought. I'm not scatting—not even on Chick's Lot. Not to the coppers. I'll get me own back, leave that ter Rocky!

"Don't know."

It generally took Mrs Flanagan a bit of time to catch up on things, but she understood the situation now.

"Yer mean our Rocky's done nothing?"

"That's right, Mrs Flanagan. Somebody has deliberately given Rocky's name to shield himself ... "

"That's what I mean—always picking on us. Yer did the same with Joey and look where he ended up. Why don't yer go after them that do get into trouble? Why don't yer leave us alone ... "

"I'm sorry, Mrs Flanagan, but we have to check on these things ... "

"Just checking! They never leave us in peace!" scolded Mrs Flanagan as they went home. "And what *were* yer doing that night, anyway?" she turned on Rocky. "Will yer never learn sense? Do you want to go the way of our Jocy?"

Rocky frowned again and hunched his shoulders.

"He started the same way. Coppers coming asking questions. And look where he is now! In jail! If yer step-father was here it wouldn't happen! I don't know why I married him, thinking he'd keep you right and then he goes off to sea again! I don't know how one woman's

35

expected to manage!" and she sank into a chair, sobbing loudly.

Rocky turned abruptly and prepared to go out, but as he reached the door, she yelled,

"And where's our Suzie?"

"Haven't seen her the day."

"Did she not go out with yer this morning?"

"I told yer—haven't seen her since."

Mrs O'Rourke sent up a wail.

"She's off again, then! We'll have to look for her! What have I done to deserve this?"

Rocky fully appreciated the situation and dashed out. Suzie was only seven and she was a queer, silent child. Some nights she crept off and stayed away till the following morning, sleeping in old houses or huts. This was the third time she'd gone missing.

Rocky ran off to go round the places Suzie might choose to hide in. He knew that Suzie went off because she was sometimes as unhappy as he was at home. They'd never talked about it, of course, but Rocky knew. When Suzie wasn't so unhappy she stuck around with Rocky everywhere, racing behind him with a crumpled bow of ribbon floating from one strand of hair six inches behind her head. But when she got really miserable, she might throw a brick through a window—or just go off like this.

"One of these days, something awful will happen to her and she won't come back!" his mother had cried, and Rocky was worried about that.

He tried the waste ground behind the Chans' shop first. There was an old air-raid shelter there. But Suzie wasn't in it. She wasn't in the disused church in St Catherine's Square, and she wasn't in the old stables.

Rocky stood still. There was one place she hadn't gone

to alone before, but she'd been there with the gang. Maybe she'd gone there alone this time. He raced off to St James's cemetery.

The old cemetery filled a deep valley that had once been a quarry. It was locked up just then, but Suzie could squeeze through anything, and she could surely get through the railings.

Rocky wandered along, peering down into the trees and bushes and shouting for her. Suddenly, he saw something red moving, and then Suzie came running up one of the long cement ramps that led to the street.

"Suzie!" Rocky said. "What a place to choose! Yer know it's dinner-time."

Suzie squeezed through the railings.

"I'm cold," she said.

Rocky took her hand and started briskly for home.

His mother was in the middle of hysterics, and all the neighbours were in. When she saw Suzie, she started up.

"Yer bad girl! Giving me all this trouble! I'll tan the hide off yer!"

Suzie hid behind her brother.

"Leave her alone, Mam. She's frightened."

"I'll frighten her!"

"Look, where's me dinner?"

"Dinner! I'll dinner yer, if yer don't let me get my hands on that child ... "

"Come on, Suzie," said Rocky, "we'll buy some chips."

Rocky raced down the Steps to Chan's, with Suzie following, her bow of ribbon bobbing behind her. With the hot packet of chips under his arm, Rocky said, "We'll eat them in the hideout, Suzie, see? It's warm there. But mind, yer have to swear never to tell anybody about it see?"

Suzie swore, unexpectedly, using a word that made Rocky open his eyes. "Who taught yer to say that?" he demanded.

Suzie gazed blankly back at him.

"Can I have me chips?"

"Yer'll've had yer chips if yer say that again, see? I mean *promise*—do yer understand, Suzie?"

Suzie nodded.

"Oh well," said Rocky, not convinced, "if it's not there yer can't put it there." A cold blast of wind came down the Steps. "Come on. We'll go to the hideout."

CHAPTER

5

THE hideout was the basement of the vicarage of St Catherine's, and Rocky had found it by forcing open the door that led from the area. Officially it was Rocky's, but it was also the gang's headquarters. They could use it for meetings and playing cards. Nobody else knew about the hideout.

Rocky never went straight into the hideout. He had worked out a cautious way of getting there which meant running past the vicarage whistling, as though you were going home or for messages, then creeping back when you were sure no one was watching, and sneaking into the area. Suzie and Rocky went through this ritual, and entered the hideout.

The main characteristics of the hideout were its darkness and its dampness and its dirt. But the gang had collected an old card table, two kitchen chairs and a stool to furnish it. Rocky had even managed to get a carpet that someone in the Square had decided to throw out. It had been beside the dustbins, and Rocky had nipped in and pinched it.

On top of the vast, black, old-fashioned range stood an old paraffin heater which had been in the house. Rocky picked it up and shook it. There was some paraffin in it still. Getting money for paraffin was a major concern of the gang. Rocky lit the stove and filled the kettle and put it on. The kettle would takes ages, of course, and the stove gave out no warmth. But the front of it glowed red and cheerful, and Rocky and Suzie sat down to eat their chips quite happily.

On the wall, the gang had stuck various postcards and pictures that had taken their fancy. There were two post-cards that Rocky had received from his father on his last voyage. Rocky often took them down and read the messages on the back—though he knew them both by heart. One was a view of the ship his father sailed in, and on the back was written: "Dear Rocky, This is the Southern Cross good ship good voyage Be a good lad Dad." The other was a picture of a big gold Buddha, and its message was: "Dear Rocky, Very hot here this fellow on the other side is the only one not sweating, Dad." When Rocky read them he could almost hear his father's voice again, speaking to him.

If you got tired of looking at the pictures, you could look out through the slits and holes in the boards over the window, and you could watch people's feet and legs as they passed—all unconscious of you. It gave you a nice safe secret feeling.

Thinking about Chick's Lot and the dirty trick they'd played Rocky grew angry again. What would his father have said about it? he wondered. He'd have gone and battered them. So would Joey, if Joey had been out. His father had told him, "Use your fists, lad. Don't let anybody put it over on yer." Yes. Use yer fists. But that hadn't been all. "Use yer fists. But use yer brains first. That's what God put them in yer head for."

"Keep yer greasy hands off them photos, Suzie," he said hastily. "Them's from the dad. Tell yer what I'll do. If yer dad sends yer any, I'll let yer stick them there as well."

An uneven step sounded on the stair outside, and then the special gang knock. It was Billy.

"Hi, Rocky," He came in, his eyes worried behind his spectacles. "The police has been to our house about that night we did the shop ... "

"I know. They took me in."

"Took yer in?" Billy was horrified. "But, Rocky ... "

"It was all right, wack. It was Chick's Lot—they framed me. They said it was me in the Terrace the night the Buildings was done. But I told the scuffers I was framed." Rocky made the tea and poured out three mugfuls. He felt a real gang-leader at last. "There's a bit of conny-milk left."

"What yer going to do, Rocky? What yer going to do ter Chick's Lot for framing yer?"

Rocky's hair seemed redder than ever, his scowl more ferocious, as he contemplated Chick's Lot and how they'd tried to frame him.

"We're going to do them—ternight."

"Yer going round to fight them?"

"Yes. Yer can pass the word along ter the gang to be ready—Joseph Terrace tonight."

Billy drank some tea. He didn't like it when the gangs fought. He didn't like it at all.

"Well, they won't be expecting us," he said. "It'll be a surprise attack."

"How much d'yer bet? They'll know I was took by the scuffers, and they'll know I've guessed. They'll be waiting all right ... "

Suzie, who had been listening with interest, came out enthusiastically with the word she'd used before.

"Honest, I'll do you, Suzie, if you say that again," threatened Rocky.

Judging that his mother would have got over her anger with Suzie by now, Rocky sent his step-sister home and went off himself to organize the gang for the evening's battle. They were enthusiastic, and arranged to meet again after dark. It was time they defeated Chick's Lot once and for all, teach them they couldn't pin their crimes on the Cats.

The gang separated for tea. Crossing the Square, Rocky saw Suzie sitting on a doorstep, her skirt wrapped up round her arms to keep them warm, watching some children skipping.

"Hi, tatty-'ead!" he called, and Suzie came running across.

"Where's yer skippie rope, then?"

Suzie looked at him with blank amazement. "Haven't got none," she said.

Rocky reflected that Suzie had never had a skipping rope that he knew of.

"Got a doll?"

Suzie shook her head. She hadn't any toys really. It was a shame.

"Tell yer what, Suzie, when I get some money I'll buy yer a doll and a skippie."

Suzie was as delighted as if the presents had already been given.

"And tell yer what, Suzie, Guy Fawkes's night we'll go and see the bonfire in Seffy Park. And Christmas, we'll go to the youth club party."

Under the influence of these cheerful things to come, Suzie and Rocky went home in good spirits.

Ellen-from-upstairs's baby was crying, and so Rocky gave her a shout as he went in, "Ellen, the baby's crying!"

"Push his dummy in his mouth, Rocky!"

"All right!"

Mrs Flanagan was sitting over the kitchen fire reading a paper-backed romance. It was her favourite occupation, and Rocky could not express the scorn he felt for these "soppy" stories.

"She has that baby out in all weathers—it's a disgrace! Yer back, are you? Going off without a word. I had messages I wanted. Ye'd better get them after tea. Well, I'll get off now. I'm going to the Launderette."

She began collecting dirty clothes from chairs and cupboards, stuffing them into a plastic bag. "Get Suzie her tea."

Rocky made some tea and cut slices of bread and margarine for Suzie and himself. There was some sausage-and-mash keeping hot in the pan and some biscuits as well. Suzie ate without a word, staring out of the window. She was sitting on the only chair at the table, and Rocky perforce ate his tea standing. The small electric fire gave off little heat, and neither Rocky nor Suzie took off their outdoor clothes. The only new object in the room was the television set. A mat, dirtied to a dull grey, lay before the hearth, the rest of the floor was covered in linoleum. The faded curtains drooped at the window, a sagging sofa was pushed against one wall, a bed which Suzie and Mrs Flanagan shared against another. A gas-stove and a sink had been fitted into a dark corner. It was a cheerless, dirty room, but neither Rocky nor Suzie paid much attention to it.

"Did she batter yer?" asked Rocky, through a mouthful.

Suzie shook her head, swinging her legs at the same time.

"What d'yer do it for, Suzie?" asked Rocky. "Why didn't yer tell me? Yer could've told me!"

Suzie shook her head again, her limp bow of ribbon flopping up and down.

Rocky scowled over the table and helped himself to a biscuit. You could get nothing out of Suzie. But she looked thinner than ever and there were dark smudges under her eyes.

"Coming to the shop, Suzie?" he asked when he'd finished. "I've got sixpence left. I'll buy yer some fizzies."

Suzie scrambled off her chair, hitched up her pants which were always drooping below her skirt, and held out her hand.

On the way, Rocky thought with satisfaction of the battle planned for that night. At least he would be showing somebody something. This time the Cats would win.

When he got back from the shops, his mother had been in, dropped the bundle of laundry, and had gone out to the bingo leaving the key with Ellen-from-upstairs. Rocky was furious. There was a note on the table saying, "Don't let Suzie out and you stay with her. Pie in cupboard for supper." Rocky rumpled his hair and gazed angrily from Suzie to the note. She couldn't be left to play out alone in case she wandered again, but he couldn't baby-sit either.

"Yer'll have to come with me to the fight, Suzie. Yer'll like that, won't yer?"

Suzie looked at him speculatively, nodded, and went on sucking her fizzies.

And so, as darkness fell, the Cats assembled in the gateway to the Buildings, prepared to do battle. They hung around waiting for little Chan, but when he didn't come, decided to go round by the fish shop and collect him. Billy followed on his tricycle, Rocky stalked ahead, and Suzie hopped in the rear, her bow precariously attached, a half-brick in her hand.

The shop was already full. Little Chan's father was frying, and his mother was serving. As Rocky stalked into the shop, he caught a glimpse of little Chan peering round the door that led to the house, but he disappeared immediately to be replaced by his four little brothers.

Mr Chan looked up at Rocky, but said nothing. Mrs Chan went on wrapping up fish and chips.

"Peter coming out?" asked Rocky at last. The Chans had always been friendly. He couldn't understand this hostility.

"Peter is going to bed early," said Mrs Chan. "Tonight he is not playing out."

Rocky scowled.

"Well, he promised he would."

"Peter has been naughty."

Rocky turned and pushed out of the shop. As he went, he heard a woman at the counter say,

"I daresay you don't want him playing with that lot from the Square. They're a rough lot."

"At first we were pleased for him to make friends," Mrs Chan explained. "But now it seems there is trouble. Policeman come asking where Peter was this night. There was trouble. We don't want him mix up in this."

"I should think not! That boy O'Rourke's going to end up like his brother."

"Who says so?" angrily Rocky shot back over his shoulder, and Suzie, seeing him upset, raised her hand to throw her half-brick through the Chans' window.

"No, Suzie!" Rocky stopped her just in time. "We'll do without Chan. Come on!"

Joseph Terrace, in spite of the new blocks of flats, always had a sinister, dark appearance and it was generally fairly deserted as though people shunned it. The Cats always approached it cautiously, partly because of its sinister atmosphere.

As they drew near the off-licence on the corner, Rocky felt his anger drain out of him as excitement filled him, prickling at the back of his neck and in his finger tips.

They had brought a few sticks to fight with, but generally they fought with their fists. Once though, Spadge had produced a knuckle-duster, and for months after that the Cats had kept clear of Chick's Lot.

The field of battle was to be the waste ground by the old houses and Chick's Lot should be hiding there in the darkness. The Cats approached cautiously. You could never tell. There might be a surprise attack.

But suddenly, dark forms moved out of the shadows. Chick's Lot were assembled, silent and threatening. The Cats stopped, and the two gangs faced each other across the waste ground with a tangible area of hatred between.

"How many of them?" Rocky murmured to the Nabber.

"Can't make out. Looks more than usual. Bet they've brought in some of the Crown Street gang."

"That's not fair!"

Rocky raised his voice.

"Hi, Chick! Who've you got helping yer?"

"Only my Lot, Kittens. Turning yeller, are yer?"

"We're not the yeller uns! How long are yer goin' to stand looking?"

"Come on, fight then!"

"Spadge got his knuckle-duster, I'll bet."

"Come and find out."

"Spadge is the yellowest," shouted the Nabber.

And suddenly the two groups of boys hurled themselves at each other. In the darkness little could be seen, but there were plenty of grunts and cries.

Billy sat on his bike at the side, frowning through his glasses, and holding Suzie firmly while she jumped up and down and shouted wildly. He wished they wouldn't fight. He just wished they wouldn't!

CHAPTER
6

BILLY couldn't make out how the battle was going, until he saw Beady stumble out of the dark mass and run towards him crying loudly.

"Hi, Beady! What's the matter?"

Beady stumbled, holding his hands to his head.

"It's that Spadge! He's gotta bicycle chain!"

He stumbled on past Billy and Billy shivered, suddenly cold. He'd seen plenty of violence, one way and another, in the streets round the flats, and he hated it. Rocky could get into awful trouble—just being in a battle with Spadge. There was a car at the far end of the Square. Whether it was a police car or not, Billy took it as an excuse. He limped over to the fight, letting Suzie go.

"Scuffers! The scuffers is here!" he yelled, and the gangs broke up, hesitating, running, shouting, "Where? Come on, lads!"

There was silence except for the pounding of feet and, at that moment, there was a crash of breaking glass. Suzie had thrown her half-brick.

"Out!" yelled Rocky, as windows in the flat opposite were flung open. Fortunately, Suzie had chosen the window of the empty shop, but even so it wasn't the time to loiter. He seized Suzie's hand and pulled her in the direction of home.

Billy, who was always slower because of the bike, was the last to reach home. The others were out of sight then. Methodically, he locked up his tricycle and slowly mounted the stairs to his flat. His mother was watching television and knitting.

"Had a good time, Billy?" she asked, as he came in.

"All right."

Billy sat down on a stool and watched the screen for a bit, but it didn't interest him and he grew restive.

"Mam, can we not move away from here?" he asked suddenly.

Mrs Griffiths stopped knitting and looked at him. Billy never said very much, but something must be wrong for him to say that.

"Why, Billy, I thought you was happy here—you've got lots of friends."

Billy frowned through his spectacles at the television screen.

"It's getting rough," he said at last.

Mrs Griffiths sighed. She knew it was. She's been so pleased at first to move into the new flat. It had nice views, and the neighbours were all right. But still …

"It's near yer dad's work, yer see," she said. "It isn't that Rocky O'Rourke got into trouble, is it?"

"Rocky's all right," said Billy stoutly. Whatever he might doubt privately about Rocky, he was all right to Billy.

And at number 3, Rocky and Suzie also sat down to watch television, Rocky in the old armchair and Suzie—all bright-eyed and grimy and tired now—on the mat. They ate a packet of crisps each as they watched.

"I belted Spadge once, anyway," Rocky reflected. "Did yer see me belt him, tatty-'ead?"

Suzie nodded without taking her eyes from the set.

"It was a good fight. It was a draw, but that was only 'cos the scuffers come and broke it up. We would have beat them otherwise. It was a good fight."

Sunday morning, the O'Rourke family got up so late, that breakfast was dinner and dinner was tea and supper didn't happen. Rocky stayed in bed, reading comics and dreaming until his mother got up. Suzie would come in with him and read her comics, or Rocky would read his to her.

Lying there, his mind going over the fight of the night before, he began to re-live it, but in much more dangerous terms. It was his gang against Chick's still, but they fought it out with guns, behind big, shiny cars, and Chick, as he lay dying, murmured to Rocky, "It's all yours now, Rocky. The set-up's all yours ..."

Rocky lived mainly in a dream world, where school and home didn't have any existence for him. In his dream world he was either a successful criminal leader or a famous footballer—it all depended where his interests lay at that moment.

After breakfast, Rocky got out of the house as soon as possible and into the freedom of the outside world where, even if it was no pleasanter than home, he was his own master.

Rocky leapt down the stairs of number 3 and across the road and on to the wall and was halfway across the Square when he remembered Beady. Beady had been a casualty last night. How badly he'd been hurt, Rocky didn't know, but maybe—his imagination took over—maybe he was even dead. Rocky stopped in his tracks. If he was, it was Spadge did it, and he would hang for it! Rocky could see himself in court, in the witness box.

"You were present on the night of this gang battle?"

"Yes."

"You saw Beady Martin shot down?"

"I did."

"You saw the man who shot him?"

"I did."

"Can you see that man in court?"

Rocky looked round, searching for Spadge's white and frightened face in the dock, but at the same time he was shouting outside the Martins' door, "Beady!" and the window shot up and Mrs Martin's angry black face appeared.

"You get away from here, Rocky O'Rourke! We don't want you around any more. You're not playing with Beady again. Getting him in fights and roughness!—You tell your mam she should be ashamed of you! Here's Beady with a big cut on his head that wouldn't stop bleeding all night!"

"Wasn't *me* hurt him!" protested Rocky, his hair bristling at the injustice.

"He was in your company!"

The window slammed, and Rocky, in a rage, did a threatening dance on the pavement, but it gave him little satisfaction. Everybody was always blaming him. Even when it was Spadge did it!

He went to the hideout, made some tea, and sat drinking it and thinking. There was no getting over the fact that Chick's Lot had done a real job and had made a lot of money out of it. Rocky would have to plan something like that. A real break-in. A big one. Then Chick and Spadge couldn't go strutting about like they were, and when Joey came home he would take Rocky about with him—introduce him to his pals and take him when he went on a job. It would mean doing a warehouse or something like that, at night. And it would need lots of planning ...

Looking up, he saw, through one of the cracks in the boards over the window, Billy limping down into the area.

"Hullo dur!" Rocky greeted him happily. "Have a

50

cupper. Help yerself. We're out of cow-juice, but. Swill some tea round the conny tin."

Billy carefully went through the ritual of pouring the tea from the old brown teapot into a tin mug, swilling some tea round the empty condensed-milk tin and pouring the reddish-brown liquid that resulted into his mug.

"What happened to Beady?" he asked.

"He only got a cut on the head—that's all. It was nothing. But you should hear the fuss his mother made! You know like, I told her to shut up. I told her it was Beady's fault if he come with us, and it was Beady's fault if he got hurt because he couldn't fight. He should be able to fight." Rocky was silent for a moment and then went on.

"Y'know like I'm thinking up the big break-in. Like we talked about. Maybe do a warehouse, or something down the docks."

"Hi, Rocky, I'm not coming in on it." Billy sounded more decided than usual.

"Yer what?" Rocky was astonished. "Will you not keep douse, like?"

Billy shook his head. Rocky was the person he admired most in life. Rocky never made fun of his limp and always treated him fair. Billy was always loyal to Rocky, but he couldn't go that far.

"I can't."

"What for? Turning chicken, are yer?"

Billy shook his head. He couldn't explain that he didn't want to be mixed up in anything like this for his mother's sake. Rocky would only pour scorn on that. So he didn't explain.

"I can't come in with youse."

Rocky regarded him with distaste, his red hair bristling.

"Honestly!" he burst out. "What a lot of wets!"

"What's the matter?" Billy was startled. "Who else's dropped out?"

Rocky didn't reply. Chan, Beady, now Billy. That left only the Nabber and himself. Well, all right then. They were the best two anyway. They'd do the break-in together.

"All right. Please yourself, wack. Only don't forget—put a trap on yer moey—no clatting to anybody about it, else we'll know who to come to!"

"Yer know I wouldn't clat, Rocky!" Billy exclaimed. "I wouldn't clat on yer—but I can't come in on it."

The rest of the gang arrived, and they sat round drinking tea and playing cards. Chan and Billy were best·at card-games, and Billy felt much happier sitting in the hideout with the others than doing break-ins or fighting other gangs. He hoped that maybe now that most of the gang didn't want those things, Rocky would forget them. But after a while, Rocky and Nabber dropped out of the game and sat whispering together. They were planning something. Billy guessed that. He heard snatches of conversation—"It'll be dead easy ter get in ... dead easy ... There's the window at the back ... Nobody would know yer were there—not once yer were through the gate."

Billy tried not to hear. If they were planning something he didn't want to know about it.

CHAPTER

7

"Hi! Scuffers! The scuffers is here!"

The message went swiftly round the boys playing in the school playground next day, and they crowded to the railings to see.

Near the main entrance, a police car was parked and two policemen were just coming into the school.

"What d'they want? Who they after?"

The Cats gathered to discuss the incident, but they were sure the police weren't after them. It could be Chick's Lot though. And during the next lesson, Rocky, seated near the window, suddenly and involuntarily stood up as he saw Spadge and Chick being shepherded into the waiting car. It took the teacher some time to quieten them again, and in fact, for the rest of the day, it was almost impossible. The news flared round the school that the two boys were arrested for the St Catherine's Buildings job. Everybody, almost, had known they'd done it, but most thought they'd get away with it.

"They tried to sell a clock to Ma Williams—she told me mam ..."

"They had a stack of money ..."

"Chick said he knew a fence ..."

The rumours went on unceasingly. Rocky was filled with a restless excitement. His thoughts went back to when Joey had been arrested. He remembered the knocking at the door, and his mother looking out of the window

and saying, "My God, there's a police car out there!"
Joey had leapt up and rushed out and tried to get away
through the back door, but they'd expected that, and
there was a scuffer waiting for him. Rocky breathed fast.
It was all exciting—all danger and excitement, and fear
at the same time.

Coming home from school that night, the Nabber and
Rocky walked behind the other three, keeping to themselves.

"Is it still on for tonight?" the Nabber asked.

"Yer not dropping out? Gone chicken because Chick
copped it?"

"Who yer kidding? I'm game if you are."

"Right. We do the place—see yer later …"

After dark that evening, the two boys met in the hideout. They blackened their faces with dirt from the stove.
The Nabber had found himself plimsolls to wear for the
occasion, and Rocky had his torch.

They had planned to get into the house of the old
woman who shouted at them at the corner of the Square.
It had been Rocky who noticed that she hadn't been
shouting for a day or two. Maybe she'd gone away.
Anyway, there'd be things worth something in there.
Mrs Flanagan had said that the old woman was called
Mrs Abercrombie, and she was rich—or she had been
once.

At first the Nabber had objected. "Doesn't look like
she's got a penny. Anyway, you know like, it's daft to do
a place close to home …"

But Rocky had persuaded him, and Rocky had also
watched the house closely. He saw no sign of Mrs Abercrombie, and never a light in the window.

"The place is empty. She's gone away. It'll be easy as

falling off a wall!" he said.

"Hi, Nabber. Have yer thought? Mebbe she's dead."

Rocky's whisper seemed to hang on the damp air between the high walls and under the dripping leaves of the narrow path that led to the back of the house. The two boys paused, considering. It was an uncomfortable thought.

"No—she'll not be dead." The Nabber moved on again, his plimsolls slipping on the damp paving-stones. They reached the back of the house. Rocky began examining the nearest window, carefully, his hands feeling round it.

"Hi, Nabber—this is open. Here, bunk us up …"

Bunked up by the Nabber, Rocky cautiously pushed open the window. The smell of house came out to him—a sour, musty, still air with all the feeling of strangeness and danger that made prickles go down your back.

"Can yer get in?"

"Yes. Keep douse …"

Rocky took a cautious look with his torch into the room and found himself about to step into the kitchen sink. He did this, and then clambered down to the floor.

The house was deathly still and silent. Flashing his torch round the kitchen, Rocky saw a large room, one wall taken up by a big old-fashioned dresser, a wooden table in the centre, old mats on the floor, a litter of dirty dishes and scraps of food. There was nothing worth lifting.

The door stood open into another room, and he squeezed carefully through. The smell of cooking didn't lie here. It was an even bigger room, with a massive dining table and chairs set round, and a big sideboard, a ghostly mirror on the wall, and everything covered in dust. Cold and still.

Moving forward, Rocky's hand brushed something on the sideboard – it toppled and fell with a crash. He froze in

55

fear, and after a moment a voice from somewhere in the house cried, "Who's that? What is it? Who's there?" The voice sounded terrified, and some of its terror was communicated to Rocky. He flashed his torch. What he'd knocked over was a small transistor radio. He seized it, stuffed it into his jacket, and made for the kitchen window, regardless now of whether he made a noise or not.

He leapt so unexpectedly down that he knocked over the Nabber, who exclaimed, "What yer doing!"

"Come on!" exclaimed Rocky, and they ran, slipping and stumbling, up the narrow pathway into the street. The Square seemed brilliantly lit after the darkness and fortunately empty. They made for the hideout.

In the hideout, they lit the lamp and examined the transistor. Rocky felt a thrill of pride. It was his first real job.

"How much d'yer think we'll get for it?" asked the Nabber.

Rocky twiddled the knobs. Nothing happened.

"It's broke!"

"Just needs new batteries."

"I'll bet. It's broke!"

"No, it's not! There—yer can hear it," Rocky insisted. "Here—she's still there. I heard her shout. You know like, we've done a real job now and when our Joey comes out we'll be able to join up with him ..."

Nabber seemed rather sceptical. "We'll see. I don't know about Joey. He got caught once ... What yer going ter do with this now?"

"There's a feller'll buy it—a fence Joey told me about. I know where to find him."

They brewed some tea and sat drinking it, seeing through the breaks in the boarded-up window St Catherine's Square, the houses thrusting roofs and chimneys up blackly into a dark grey sky.

Rocky felt some of his excitement subsiding. He'd done it. At last.

As they scrubbed the dirt off their faces, he said,

"You know like, Nabber, me mam's off ter see our kid tomorrow and I'm sagging school. Are yer coming? We can go down to the landing-stage and find the fence. What d'yer think he'll give us for the transistor?"

"I thought yer wanted ter keep it?"

"Well, I want one, but if I could get some money it would be better ..."

"All right. We'll go tomorrow."

CHAPTER

8

"Eh dear," said Mrs Flanagan, sitting in the armchair in her curlers and old coat and drinking tea. "I've got the intuition something awful."

Rocky who was standing at the table, full of irritation that his mother hadn't yet got herself off to see Joey, stopped chewing his jam butty and looked at her. Her words sent a prickle down his spine. Mrs Flanagan's intuition was well known in her family—it never failed. If she felt something was going to happen—it happened.

Rocky swallowed and looked at Suzie who was sitting on the chair eating her breakfast and also gazing at Mrs Flanagan in fascination.

"What yer got the intuition about then?" asked Rocky.

Mrs Flanagan turned to stare at him with that faraway gaze which she adopted on these occasions and which made Rocky's blood curdle still further.

"I don't know. But I dreamed of our Joey last night. I hope he's not in more trouble!"

Rocky thought of Jimmy Simpson straight away. Joey would be in more trouble if he came out of prison and Jimmy Simpson's gang got on to him. He must warn Joey—as soon as he got home.

Mrs Flanagan yawned and picked up the alarm clock, shaking it so that it rattled as though all its innards were loose—which they were.

"This old clock. If it had gone off this morning I would

have been on the early bus. What's the matter with it?"

Rocky wriggled into his coat irritably. Why didn't she get herself off. It was always the same. It took her ages to get anywhere, and she was upsetting all his plans.

"Yer knew it was broke."

"I didn't. Who broke it?"

"It's been broke for ages."

"Well I didn't know. Doesn't matter, anyway. I'll catch the ten o'clock train. I'll be a bit late for Joey, but so long as I see him that's what counts. Has that girl gone ter school? Did yer give her face a rub, Rocky? She's as black as a coal bin."

"Hi, Mam, I need a new pair of sandals. Look." Rocky lifted his right foot to display a hole right through the sole of his sandal.

"Yer shouldn't wear them out so quickly. All this running about …"

"Well, what'm I going ter do, Mam?"

"I don't know. I don't know where the money goes. Ye'll have to wait a bit. Put some newspaper in just now …"

Rocky was furious, but there was nothing else to be done. "Me feet get all wet," he grumbled. Then, "If I sell the transistor, I'll buy meself some shoes. And not Jesus-boots, neither—proper shoes," he thought.

"Stop muttering ter yerself, Rocky. Yer get on my nerves!" She went over to the mirror above the fireplace, taking out her curlers, combing her hair, putting on the strongly smelling make-up she used.

"What yer hanging about for? Are yer not going to school today or something?"

Rocky's heart leapt for a moment as he thought she'd guessed he was sagging school. But it wasn't that. He could tell by the way she went on with her lipstick.

"I have to have the key, haven't I?"

"Oh yes. I forgot."

"And if yer not quick, I'll be late for school ..."

They left the house together. His mother handed him the keys as they parted.

"Now mind, none of that crowd in while I'm away. And give Suzie her tea. She'll get her dinner at school, and you get yours there ..."

Mrs Flanagan went off towards Upper Parliament Street, and Rocky raced along the wall towards the Steps where the Nabber was waiting.

"So ye've come, mate! I thought I'd sagged school for nothing. Here's the transistor. Yer want ter carry it?"

Rocky stuffed it down the front of his jerkin, and together they started off on the road down to the docks. They sang as they went and fooled round, filled with exhilaration at playing truant and at the bright, frosty air that nipped their faces. They waited near the curve of the steep bank up from the docks, where the lorries had to move slowly, and when a likely one came by they climbed on the back.

It made you sweat, that did. You had to watch out for the scuffers, and for the driver seeing you. And then, if the lorry accelerated suddenly, you might get thrown off. When you were on, you kept low down, so you wouldn't be seen, and then you took whatever there was. That day, they got packets of biscuits, slitting open a cardboard box full of them, and taking as many as they could carry. When the lorry stopped at the traffic lights in Renshaw Street, they dropped off the back.

Then they swaggered along, eating biscuits, and thinking they were very clever fellows. Rocky talked to the Nabber then about the big break-in he was planning, and they wandered round the streets of Liverpool looking for a place to break into. They acted very mysteriously and suspiciously, and more than one store manager conducted them out into the street to get them off the premises.

Gradually, they made their way to Pier Head, where the ferries across the Mersey came in to the floating landing stage. They were both cold and hungry by that time.

The Mersey was grey and cold and choppy, and the wind blew gustily and damply across it.

"There's the New Brighton ferry in. If we had the money we could go down there."

"Well we haven't the money. I've got sixpence."

"I've got a shilling."

"Not enough."

"We'll go into the snack bar. Maybe the fence'll be there and I'll sell him this—come on."

The long narrow room was hot and crowded; the windows steamed against the cold outside.

Nudging each other and laughing with excitement, the two boys pushed their way through the crowd.

"What's he look like?"

"He's a little old feller with a black bowler hat and a red hankie in his top pocket. He's called Old Jake."

"Well, he's not here, wack."

"Well Joey said he generally was."

"Well Joey's wrong, in't he?"

"Now then, you two lads, stop fooling about. What d'yer want?" asked a woman behind the counter.

"What jer got?" asked the Nabber.

"None of yer cheek."

"We'll have a bowl of soup and a bun," said Rocky. "We've got enough for that," he added to the Nabber. "Grab a couple of spoons and we'll share it."

They broke the bread into the soup, and ate it together—
a spoon at each side.

"Yer see that, wack?" Rocky nudged the Nabber, in-
dicating an old man mumbling over a cup of coffee in the
corner. "He's a nut case."

"Maybe he's not well."

"Go on! He's nuts, or he's lushed. He's always here.
He's a lush. He's always drunk."

Suddenly Rocky froze. "Hi, Nabber. Yer see that?"

"What is it?"

Rocky was staring out of the window at two men who
were approaching.

"It's Jim Simpson! Hi, Nabber, that's Jim Simpson—
look!"

"Shurrup! Yer'll start a riot!"

Rocky bent over his soup, quite mistakenly suspecting
that Jim Simpson would know him immediately and seek
him out. Jim Simpson, in a heavy, rough tweed coat and
expensive leather gloves, pushed his way straight through
the crowds to the lush, who looked up myopically at him.
They sat at the table talking confidentially.

"He's not half big. He's that tall he could wring the
Liver birds' necks," said Rocky.

"He's big all right. He hasn't got his gang with him, but."
The Nabber took a cautious look at him.

Rocky snorted derisively. "He's a big-head. Gorra a
head as big as Birkenhead. Thinks he owns the place.
Thinks he's Lord Liverpool ..."

"Well he's not a nobody," said the Nabber. "The
coppers never got him yet."

A strong desire was growing in Rocky to get into closer
contact with his brother's enemy—find out something he
could pass on to Joey.

"Hi, I'm going over," he said.

"Don't be soft—what for?"

"Find out what they're talking about. You stay here …"

Rocky edged over towards them, trying to hear what they were discussing. It would help Joey if he could find out. Because maybe they were talking about Joey …

But he had just got beside them, when Jim Simpson looked up.

"What d'yer want, lad?" he asked. "After something?"

"You know like …" Rocky thought fast. "You know like, I've lost me bus fare home …"

Rocky was conscious only of a pair of prominent blue eyes in a fleshy face that looked him over carefully, trying to place him.

"That's likely—but here yer are." He took a shilling from his pocket. "Haven't I seen you before somewhere?"

"Thank you very much, mister. No, mister. Don't think so. Terrah!"

Rocky gave the Nabber a nod as he hurried out, and the Nabber came dashing out after him.

"Hi, what'd he say to yer? Did yer hear anything?" the Nabber yelled as they raced across the bridge and towards the bus stop.

Rocky didn't reply till they were seated breathlessly on the top deck.

"He give's this …"

"A shilling!" The Nabber was scornful. "That all?"

"No, it wasn't, see. He said he knew me—he knew I was Joey's brother," said Rocky, dramatizing the situation. "He said he knew who I was and ter tell Joey he was out to get him. And he said for me ter keep out of his way or he'd get me as well!"

The Nabber reflected on this for some moments in a cynical silence. Then he said, "Who yer codding, like …?"

"I'm not codding! He did say that!"

"Go on!"

"I'll hang one on you, Nabber, calling me a liar!"

"You and who else?"

"If youse two boys want a fight, let's know and I'll clear the bottom platform for it. Otherwise, youse gets off next stop," said the conductor. "And where's yer fares?"

His mother was already home, drinking tea and looking aggrieved.

"Where've yer been, me lad? I come home and the house is empty. How d'yer expect me to get in? I've had to climb through the back window!"

"What about Joey, Mam? When's he coming out?"

"Well, me intuition was right—it was our Joey. He's been a good lad and they're letting him out early. He's coming tomorrow!"

"Well yer intuition was wrong, wasn't it?"

"No it wasn't. Doesn't always need ter be something bad happening." She looked at Rocky with sudden suspicion. "And where've you been till this time? Ellen-from-upstairs had to take our Suzie in because *you* couldn't be found. Where d'yer get to, I'd like ter know?"

"I was with Nabber."

Rocky had drawn near the electric fire, glad to be near some warmth again. His face and hands began to burn with the change from the cold air outside.

"When Joey comes back will he sleep in my bed again like he used to?"

"Where else would he sleep?" Mrs Flanagan yawned. "That trip fair tires me out ..."

Mrs Flanagan sat nodding in her chair, falling asleep. Suddenly Rocky found the silence of the room oppressive. He was relieved when there was a loud thump from upstairs and Ellen's baby began crying. His mother did not wake up.

His thoughts went back to the transistor which he'd hidden in the hideout for safety. It was a good transistor, but now that he hadn't been able to sell it, the thought of it stayed in the back of his mind, oppressing him and making him restless. It brought the old woman into his mind as well, and he found himself worrying in case she was really ill. Why hadn't she told the police he'd been in the house last night?

Unable to settle, he went quietly out of the room, leaving his mother asleep. The cold and darkness of the Square revived his spirits, and he went round calling on the gang to come to the hideout. They could play cards and he could show them the transistor.

"Where'd yer get it, Rocky?" asked Billy.

"I did a job."

"Yer mean yer nicked it?"

"I'm not admitting ter nothing."

Billy played a card in silence, but little Chan said, "It is a bad thing to steal what belongs to somebody else."

"Ah go on!" said the Nabber. "Who knows about it?"

"*We* all know," said little Chan. "My father says it is a sin to steal. You begin with a penny, and you end up with a thousand pounds."

Rocky glared at him. "That's the whole idea – honestly! Some people! Yer mean yer haven't seen *that* yet? Anyway, yer came in on the first break-in, didn't you?"

"Yer know Chick and Spadge's been sent away? Chick's mam came home crying from the court."

The boys reflected on this. Rocky knew all about the scenes that followed on a boy's being sent away. He'd seen it happen a lot with Joey.

"I would be careful, Rocky," said Billy. "I wouldn't flash it around—the transistor, I mean …"

"I can watch out fer meself, thanks! 'Ere, that's my trick, and yer owe me threepence, Beady!"

But when the gang went, he still felt restless. And he didn't want to leave the transistor in the hideout either. It was his now—or half his. When Joey came home, he would tell him where he could sell it, then he'd split the money with the Nabber. But till then, he would use it.

To take his mind off it, he wandered off towards the pub in Joseph Terrace. Now that Chick and Spadge had gone, the territory was free to the Cats, and he hoped he might see the wingy. He liked chatting to the wingy because he didn't treat him like a kid.

As he walked, he switched on the transistor and held it to his ear.

Under the light above the door of the pub, Mr Oliver was talking to another man. As Rocky approached, they separated and Mr Oliver came down the steps towards him. For once he seemed sober.

"Hello, Rocky! How's tricks?"

"All right, Mr Oliver."

They stood together at the corner, watching the sparse night life of Joseph Terrace.

"Good match this afternoon, Rocky. Did yer hear Everton beat Chelsea?"

"I heard it, Mr Oliver—on the transistor."

"Yer did? Coming up in the world, aren't yer? Where'd yer get that from?"

"It was—do yer want to hear it?"

"Go on then—only don't wake the neighbours …"

Engrossed in finding a programme, Rocky didn't notice Constable McMahon approaching on his beat until the policeman had stopped beside them. Then he switched the radio off, but he knew the constable had seen it.

"Hello, Davey. How's life?" asked McMahon.

"Not so bad. How's yerself? Not a fit night for a dog ter be out, is it?"

"It is not. And that lad looks frozen through. It's Rocky O'Rourke, isn't it? That wouldn't be a transistor you've got there, would it?"

"What if it is?"

"Yours, is it?"

Rocky nodded. Suddenly his mouth was too dry for him to speak.

"Mind if I have a look?"

Reluctantly, Rocky handed it over and stood waiting for the questions to start. Constable McMahon examined it closely, then stood with it in his hands.

"All right. Just checking up, yer know. There was transistors taken from the Buildings that time, but not one of this make."

"Oh, Rocky's not a thief, aren't yer not, Rocky? He's a footballer."

"So long as he keeps to it. Where d'you get it?" He handed it back, and Rocky clutched it thankfully.

"Me mam. She had a win on the bingo."

"She'd have done better to have bought yer some warm clothes—an' a pair of shoes," said the policeman.

"Me shoes is all right," muttered Rocky defiantly. The thing he had against Mr Oliver was his friendship with the police—calling them Mac, and Sarge, and Fred.

"They're all right, Rocky," he would say. "They're just doin' a job. Now somebody has to keep the rules, haven't they? Stands ter reason, doesn't it?"

But Rocky couldn't be persuaded to that point of view. They'd taken Joey away. That was enough.

"Sure it was yer mam gave it to yer?" repeated the

67

constable.

Rocky went cold. He was still suspicious, the scuffer.

"I said so, didn't I? Think I'm telling lies? It's always the same. Like me mam says, it doesn't pay ter tell the truth—you'll not be believed ..."

Something in Rocky's voice woke the wingy up to the fact that there was trouble somewhere and, not understanding but wanting to support Rocky, he said, "That's right, Mac, that's right. It was his mother. She told me herself."

"She did?" The constable sounded surprised, and looked steadily at Mr Oliver.

"Aye." The wingy looked away. "She did."

"All right, Davey. I'll believe yer," said Constable McMahon, meaningly. "And I won't forget ..."

He paced off down the Terrace.

Rocky and the wingy watched him go, past the pub, past the shops due for demolition, past the off-licence and round the corner. A fine rain was drizzling down now, and grey, misty clouds lay heavily over the city. Opposite them, the archway into the Buildings was dark, and light after light came on in the flats above.

"So, Rocky," said the wingy, who suddenly seemed very sober, "he was right, was he? Old Mac seems to know yer better than me."

"What d'yer mean ... ?"

"I mean, Rocky, yer nicked that radio set, didn't yer?"

"Honest, Mr Oliver, honest ... " Rocky began to protest.

"Come off it, lad, I wasn't born yesterday ..." Mr Oliver turned and began walking away. Rocky stood in the doorway of the pub, still clutching the radio, but with a feeling of loneliness and depression. Mr Oliver was giving him up.

But suddenly, the wingy turned and came striding back, his right hand gesticulating fiercely at Rocky.

"I'm telling yer, lad ... just you listen ter me! It's not the lorry-skipping, like, or the hanging around Lime Street Station picking up coppers ..."

Rocky was amazed. "How d'yer know I goes ..."

"Look, lad, I did the same meself when I was a kid. It's kid's stuff. Well it is, isn't it? I mean, yer don't find grown men doing it, do yer?"

"Well, no, leastways I haven't seen em," Rocky conceded reluctantly.

"Not likely to neither! But all right—we'll ferget *that*. Yer'll grow out of it. And when yer comes to me and says, 'Mr Oliver, I've give up the lorry-skipping. It's a mugs' game,' I'll say to you, 'Rocky, wack, shake hands. Yer a man!' That's what I'll say. But *this—this* sort of business!"

With another wave of disgust the wingy turned and stalked away again, only to return once more, still gesticulating.

"Yer know where it ends? I mean, apart from the rights and wrongs on it. Yer know where it gets yer? In the clink!"

"No it doesn't—no it ..."

"Doesn't it? What about yer kid brother? What about Chick and Spadge?"

"They was ..."

"Fools—idiots!" His voice dropped. "Listen, Rocky. You learn sense, lad, and I'll do more'n shake yer hand. I'll ... I'll ..." Ideas failed him, and he came up with the only thing he could think of, "I'll buy yer a pint!"

"But I don't ... Me mam wouldn't let me ..."

"And just think, Rocky. I don't suppose yer pinched that off anybody as could afford ter lose it, did yer? Yer got it off somebody who's missing it right now and hasn't the money to replace it! Ah shurrup, Rocky! Wake up ter yerself!"

The wingy swung round and was off, charging away through the night towards the Buildings. Rocky, left by himself, was trembling, suddenly cold and miserable and indignant all at once.

"Who does he think he is?" he asked himself, and then yelled, "Who d'yer think yer are? Me granny?"

He began to run home, skirting round the Buildings, and not wanting to see the wingy again. It was *his* transistor. No matter what he said. It was his and he was keeping it.

But in the Square, he hesitated. A whole jumble of thoughts and feelings confused him. McMahon had seen him with it. The wingy thought nothing of him for taking it, and maybe the old woman there was missing it …

Rocky turned disconsolately towards the old woman's house.

CHAPTER
9

IF I could just, thought Rocky, just leave it on the step, maybe. Or shove it through the window.

He didn't want to go into the dark house again, especially since there was no Nabber with him to keep douse and bunk him up. He didn't fancy that narrow path all by himself either.

Passing his own home, he saw the light was on and through the curtains that never closed properly he could see his mother moving about. He'd get rid of the transistor quickly. He pushed open the gate of the old woman's house and walked through the garden. The house was silent, there were no lights.

Rocky mounted the two steps to the door and then hesitated. Finally he rang the bell. There was no response. He pushed the door and, surprisingly, it swung back with a loud creak, and a cold breeze brought the smell of the house to him from a dark hallway—damp and dirt—smells he was well accustomed to.

"Who's that? Who's there?" a voice screamed from inside. Rocky recognized the fear in it—he was almost as afraid himself.

Rocky stood still, his eyes growing accustomed to the darkness of the hall. If he could find a place to put the transistor down, he would drop it and run. But to his horror, as he hesitated, the door at the end of the hall swung slowly open and an old woman in a long nightdress tottered out.

Seeing him, the woman screamed again and that frightened Rocky more than anything.

"Here, shurrup dur!" he shouted. "Yer'll have the scuffers in!"

"Go away! Get out! Help!"

Rocky started forward in alarm, and the old woman collapsed and fell against the wall.

"Here, missus—ye're all right? Here, missus, I don't mean yer no harm." Frightened by her white face, closed eyes and the stillness, Rocky went on wildly, "Yer see, it was just to return the transistor—I pinched it from yer last night, but I've brought it back now and I want yer ter know ..."

The old woman stirred and opened her eyes. One hand stretched out and grasped Rocky's arm.

"Help—help me ..."

Rocky helped her to her feet and into the room. There was a bed-light burning and an untidy bed pushed in among the huge, old-fashioned furniture of a sitting room. There was dust and cobwebs everywhere.

The old woman lay down again, and pulled the blankets over herself.

"Who are you? What d'you want?"

"I'm Rocky O'Rourke—I live at number 3. Look, I don't mean any harm. I just wondered if yer was all right?"

"I'm not—I'm sick. I'm very sick," said the old woman, and began to cry.

Rocky watched her desperately.

"Will I get the doctor ter yer?"

"No, no—I don't want a doctor. He'll have me taken away ... Can you get me a drink of water? There's a cup on the table—the kitchen's down the passage ..."

"I know ..." Rocky pulled up short. "I'll find it."

Apart from the light beside the old woman's bed, Rocky couldn't find any others that worked, but he groped his way to the kitchen and got the water. The old woman drank it eagerly, and lay down again.

"Tell yer what," said Rocky, "I could make yer a cup of tea."

"There's nothing in the house ... No tea, nothing ... The gas is off ..."

"Here, just a minute ... I'll get yer something ..."

Rocky departed, full of his mission. He ran to his own den, made a kettleful of tea, and took it back with the conny milk and a piece of pie that happened to be there. The old woman drank the tea, but wouldn't eat the pie.

Rocky stood watching her. She seemed to have forgotten his confession about the transistor, and he wasn't going to remind her. She looked like somebody coming out of a deep sleep.

"It's kind of you—to bother. Who are you?" she asked, again.

"I'm Rocky O'Rourke. I live at number 3 ... Look, I'll have to get back home."

"Yes, yes, it must be late ..." The old woman's voice faded, and she looked round her with dazed, frightened eyes.

"Listen, missus. If yer like, I'll come in termorrow and get yer messages. All right?"

"That's kind. But, I'm so cold ..."

Rocky ran back to the hideout to fill a hot-water bottle, and before he finally left the old woman was almost asleep.

In the darkness of the garden, Rocky stood still. What was the Nabber going to say? After all, the transistor was half his. "Ah well," he thought, "I'm the boss of this outfit anyway, aren't I? If the boss can't do what he likes it's a bad job ..."

73

When Rocky got home from school the following evening, the house showed signs of preparation for Joey's homecoming. Mrs Flanagan had bundled all the dirty clothes and old newspapers into the bottom of a cupboard, and she'd actually put a cloth on the table and a vase of artificial flowers on it. Rocky was impressed.

"Hi, mam, that's smashing! Are we having a party for our Joey?"

"I should think he'll need one! Anyway, he'll have to have a good meal. Now go and get some messages before Richardson's closes."

For once Rocky did not object.

"I want a quarter of boiled ham and a packet of cigarettes and a swiss roll and a bottle of lemonade," Rocky chanted.

"All right, all right—sniff—having a party?"

"Our Joey's back tonight ... He'll be home now, I should think ..."

And going home again, he found Suzie standing lost and prepared for flight beside the newsagent's.

"Come on, tatty-'ead. We're having a party. Joey's back."

"Don't like Joey."

"Yer've never met Joey. He's smashin'. Come on—I've got a bottle of lemonade ... Just a minute till I get the *Lion*."

Rocky collected his comic and came out immersed in it, the basket slung from his arm. He found his way through the square by instinct, not sight.

"There's another lot of footballer's pictures in it for me album. Look, tatty-'ead. Here, you carry them, in case I drop them. Here, look what's happening to the Carson's Cubs this week ... Hi."

"What they doin', Rocky?"

"They took castor-oil for their stomach ache – and see, they won the footy match after all ... It says here the Irish

74

played at Anfield and lost seven ter nil—but that was a long time ago ..." At home again, he shouted, "I've got them, Mam. Is he back?"

"Back? He is not. Where's he got to? He's missed the six bus and he can't get another till nine. I don't know. It'll be ten before he's here, I shouldn't wonder."

"Can we have a drink of lemonade now?"

"Go on, then. But not all of it."

In fifteen minutes, Mrs Flanagan was saying, "Well I'm not sitting in here till ten o'clock for him. I'm off ter see Mrs Thompson for an hour."

Rocky decided he would go to the youth club. If Joey wasn't coming home till late, it would fill in the time. He would leave early just to make sure. But first, he'd better call on Mrs Abercrombie.

The need to call again on Mrs Abercrombie had been something of a shadow over Rocky that day. He knew he'd have to see how she was, but on the other hand, remembering how ill she'd been, he rather feared calling again in case she had died. Rocky had a deep-seated fear of death and possible ghosts which his mother had fostered.

He loitered about the Square, trying to get his courage up to the point, when Billy came along on his bike, looking rather lost and lonely, for the gang seemed to have fallen apart lately, and Billy missed Rocky's friendship. None of the others had much time for Billy since he couldn't get around as they could.

"Hi, Billy! How are yer, wack? Where yer off to?"

"Nowhere. Just ridin' round."

"Here, Billy, our Joey's coming back tonight. Me mam's having a party for him."

An idea suddenly occurred to Rocky. He would take Billy to see Mrs Abercrombie. Billy could be trusted to keep his mouth shut, and it would mean he wouldn't go

75

into the house alone.

"Hi, wack. Come on with me."

"Where?"

"Have to see somebody—yer know the old woman who shouts at yer? I'm doing some messages for her ..."

"O.K."

Billy left his bike outside and followed Rocky into the house, a little worried at this freedom of entry, but prepared to trust Rocky, who went through the hall shouting, "Mrs Abercrombie! Are yer all right? It's me — Rocky."

Rocky did not go into her room until he heard her voice weakly answering, "Come in, come in, Rocky."

She was lying in bed, and to Rocky she seemed worse than she'd been the night before.

"How are yer, missus?"

"I'm cold, Rocky. Can yer fill the bottle for me?"

And then she noticed Billy standing just inside the door, frowning, and feeling worried.

"Who's that?"

"He's all right. That's Billy—Billy Griffiths. He's my pal. Here, Billy, can yer go down the hideout and boil the kettle and make some tea in this flask and fill the bottle here?"

Billy, frowning even more, nodded and departed.

Left alone with the old woman again, and watching her thin, pale face with the strangely bright eyes fixed on him, Rocky began to feel uneasy.

"Yer want any messages, Mrs Abercombie, 'cos I'll get them before I go ter the youth club."

Mrs Abercrombie shook her head. Her mouth seemed to be dry, and she constantly passed her tongue over her lips. "Could you get me some water?"

"Yer want any messages, Mrs Abercrombie, 'cos I'm going to the youth club tonight," he repeated, bringing the water to her.

Mrs Abercrombie shook her head again, and drank. Then she lay back again.

"What's it like outside?" she asked suddenly.

"It's that wet yer could do with webbed feet," said Rocky, cheerfully wiping his nose on the back of his hand, "and it's cold ..."

"Have you no stronger shoes than those, Rocky?"

Rocky looked down at his grey and soaking Jesus-boots.

"Not just now. I had some boots once, but yer grow out of them, you know. And I had a pair of shoes about a year ago ..." he looked reflective. A year ago. He'd been bought them when his mother married again. "Anyway— me mam had ter sell them when we was short once."

Mrs Abercrombie looked thoughtful. She had some shoes in the house. They'd belonged to her son—and there were some of her husband's, though they'd be too big for Rocky. But the others ... if she could remember where they were ... But her memory was so bad these days, and she hadn't the energy to go and look.

Rocky pulled a packet of biscuits from his jacket:

"Some biscuits for yer ..."

"That's a lot of biscuits, Rocky," said Mrs Abercrombie. "Not that they're not good biscuits, but there's a lot of them."

"Got them from an old fellow—down the docks. He had a lot," the lie came glibly from Rocky's lips. He couldn't understand Mrs Abercrombie worrying about such things. His mother accepted whatever he brought into the house without question. She was even careless about it. Only the other morning Suzie nearly brought trouble on him by being observed by Constable McMahon as she wandered along Princes Boulevard with a full packet of biscuits in one hand, which she was steadily eating her way through. In her usual fashion, she refused to answer questions, and was led back to number 3 by the constable.

"Looked as though she was making off again," he'd told Mrs Flanagan. "I thought I recognized the signs. Where d'you think she got those biscuits from?"

"Well, I never know where they get things from, but then that's life, isn't it?"

Billy came back in time to hear Rocky's explanation about the source of the biscuits. He guessed where they'd really come from, but didn't say anything.

The two boys stood watching the old woman as she drank some tea and ate a biscuit.

"You know like," said Billy, "you should get a doctor to her."

"I don't want a doctor," said Mrs Abercrombie. "He'll have me taken away. He won't get a doctor, will he, Rocky?"

"Well," said Billy, "the weather forecast says it'll be cold the night. She should have a fire."

"I'll leave the paraffin heater on for you, missus," said Rocky. "So you won't feel cold. And I'll be in the morrer ..."

"All right, Rocky. All right. Thank you, Rocky."

Outside, Rocky said, "Will yer come with me to-morrow to see her, Billy? If she's no better, I'd better tell somebody—maybe our kid."

"O.K."

"Coming to the club, Billy?"

"No. Have to get home."

The two boys separated, Billy cycling towards the flats, Rocky making for the church hall.

He bounded into the light and noise of the Baptist hall, and pushed his way to the counter where they were serving tea and biscuits.

"Hi, buy's a cup a tea, will yer?" he asked a boy. "I've forgot me money."

"Buy yer own, mate!"

"Hi, Betty," he said to the girl behind the counter— Betty Mulloney, a girl from the Square, "let's have a cup and I'll pay next week—I've forgot me money."

"Yer'll have ter ask Mr Cooper."

"Mr Cooper, can I ..."

"All right, Rocky. You can have it. And what's the excitement about tonight then?"

"It's me brother Joey—he's coming tonight."

"Been to sea has he?"

"No, he's been in jail."

Rocky grinned proudly over his cup of tea. "I'll have ter leave early tonight, yer see,' cos I want to be home when he comes."

And finally, on his way back, he saw the wingy, just leaving the pub, and dashed across to him.

"Mr Oliver! Hi, Mr Oliver ..."

"Rocky—what are you up to?"

"Mr Oliver, I wanted ter tell yer—our Joey's back tonight. And, Mr Oliver—I took that transistor back."

"I'm pleased at that, Rocky. Shake hands on it." He shook Rocky's hand, and left a coin in the palm.

"Mr Oliver—half a crown!"

"Is it? I thought it was a penny. Never mind. I promised yer a pint, didn't I?"

The wingy didn't seem so happy. Rocky wondered what was wrong.

"Yer going home now, Mr Oliver?"

"Yes, Rocky. Not that it'll be home much longer. I've lost me job. They're moving me out."

"Lost yer job? But what for?"

"People complaining. They say I don't do the job, and I drink too much. Honestly! It's this holier than thou attitude that gets me!" he exclaimed. "Anyway, the wife's upset. Take warning from me, Rocky. Have two strings ter yer bow. I only had one—I was a footballer, and when I wasn't that, I was nothing ..."

Rocky watched him walking slowly away, shaking his head. It was a pity about Mr Oliver.

He would go home. His mother would be out and Joey wouldn't be back till ten, but he'd go home and wait for them.

On the way he bought a packet of chips, and in a slightly happier frame of mind he entered number 3, whistling to himself as he pushed open the living-room door.

He pulled up short at the sight of the figure sitting in the old chair reading an evening paper, who looked up and said,

" 'Ullo there, Rocky! I was wondering where everybody was. 'Ere, you've put on an inch or two since I last seen yer, haven't yer?"

"Joey! Are yer just out?"

"Just this minute, Rocky, just this minute! How are yer, skin!" and he playfully cuffed Rocky's ear.

Rocky dodged back. "What was it like, Joey?"

"Not bad, lad. Not bad. Here, where's our mam?"

"She's out. With Mrs Thompson. Mrs Thompson's 'er friend, now."

"Oh lord! Mam and her friends! Nothing's changed."

Rocky was disappointed. He hadn't expected Joey's homecoming to be like this—there was something flat and wrong about everything. On the table, the cloth spread for Joey's return looked limp. The thin, pink slices of ham were dried and curling.

"We thought you would come earlier. We were going

to have a party—do yer not want something to eat?"

Joey glanced at the feast casually. He seemed restless and uneasy. "No thanks, skin. I had a meal." He lit a cigarette, glancing at his watch.

"Yer gonna get yer own back on Jim Simpson now, Joey? I saw him ... "

"Saw him? Where?"

"Well, down at the lanny ... "

"Oh there. He was always around there."

"But he was up here as well. He was asking Pa Richardson if yer were out yet ... "

Joey became still, his eyes fixed on the electric fire, the paper slipping from his knee.

"He asked that, did he?"

"Pa Richardson didn't tell him nothing ... "

Joey stood up.

"I'll have ter go, skin. Have ter see a man before ten, about a job. Has me mam any money put away?"

"What?"

"Me mam—has she any money?"

"In the old teapot—but I think it's the house-keeping ... "

Joey got up, picked up the teapot and extracted several pound notes.

"Yer can't take that, Joey. Joey, if yer steal off yer mam yer hand'll wither."

Joey laughed.

"That's an old wives' tale. Anyway, I'm only borrow-ing. Listen, wack. I'll have to go. Got business to see to. Tell me mam I'll see 'er some time."

"But Joey!"

The door slammed behind him. Rocky blinked in amazement. "She'll think *I've* pinched the money!" he said.

Something stirred behind the sofa and Suzie's head appeared. "Who was that?" she asked. "Has he gone?"

"Suzie! What yer hiding for? That was our kid—our Joey!"

"I don't like him!"

Rocky moved disconsolately to the table. He was disappointed. There'd been no party, and Joey seemed different somehow, not full of life and jokes like he'd been. Still, he probably had things to see to.

"Yer'll like him when yer get ter know him, tatty-'ead. Here, want some of this?"

They stood by the table, helping themselves to slices of ham and swiss roll with their fingers. Rocky poured out cups of lemonade.

"Smashin', isn't it?"

Suzie nodded, her mouth full of ham.

"When yer dad comes we'll have a party—a proper party, eh?"

"When's me dad coming?"

"I don't know. Soon, I expect … "

Much later, when Rocky was asleep in bed, the light was switched on, and he opened his eyes sleepily to see his mother.

"Rocky! Where's our Joey? Did he not come?"

"Yes, Mam, he come. But he's gone again."

"Where's he gone?"

"Don't know. He took the money out of the teapot … "

He fell asleep with the sound of his mother's lamenting in his ears.

CHAPTER
10

ROCKY got up next morning feeling nothing was right with his world, and it did seem that from the time of Joey's disappearance nothing *was* right. Mrs Flanagan had decided she wasn't well enough to get up, and lay on the bed in the living-room in a worse temper than usual.

"Thought yer said our Joey was back!" she grumbled.

"Well he is. I saw him. And the money's gone, hasn't it? Suzie, if yer don't stop that I'll lay into yer," for Suzie was also in a perverse mood and sat at the table throwing bits of bread about the room.

"Where's he now then?"

"How should I know? He didn't tell me." Privately he thought Joey was settling with Jimmy Simpson.

"I don't know. What a way ter go on. It's upset me proper."

"Rocky! Yer coming?"

It was Billy shouting from outside, and Rocky suddenly remembered his obligations to Mrs Abercrombie. He stuck his head out of the window.

"Just a sec." And to his mother, "Have I not got another shirt, mam? The teacher said I had ter have a clean one. She said this was mucky."

"She said what?" Mrs Flanagan rose in her bed, a picture of outraged decency. "She said *what*?"

Rocky saw there'd be no clean shirt coming, only

trouble. Suzie also recognized the signs and scrambled down from the chair.

"Oh never mind. I'll put it on again. Come on, tatty-'ead!"

"You get off ter school, Suzie," he said, outside. "Billy and me'll follow. Come on!"

There was a frost that morning that, mingled with the petrol fumes from Catherine Street, caught in your throat and nipped your nose and fingers immediately.

Rocky thrust his hands into his pockets, hunched his shoulders, and went off with a peculiar dancing gait as the cold struck through his thin sandals from the pavement.

"Hi, Rocky, not so fast."

"All right, Billy. Here, d'yer think she'll be all right?"

Billy shrugged, his downcast face suggesting that he never expected anything particularly good from this world.

Rocky pushed the door open and they stepped into the hall that seemed to have an added stillness that morning.

"Hi there! Mrs Aber! Are yer there?"

There was no reply.

Rocky and Billy exchanged glances, then Rocky went quickly along the hall. Cautiously he pushed open the door and peered in. Mrs Abercrombie lay quite still. In the dimness of the curtained room, her face looked strangely white and drawn.

"Hi, Billy. I think she's had it," said Rocky. "Look, skin, belt off on yer bike, will yer, and get the wingy. Me mam's in bed—no good getting her … "

Billy limped off, and Rocky took another look at the old woman.

"Mrs Abercrombie."

A slight moan from the bed. Rocky gulped with relief. Well, at least she wasn't dead. He went back to the garden and then to the gate, wondering whether he shouldn't go after the wingy himself and hurry things up.

But passing the gate, Constable McMahon stopped and looked down at Rocky who seemed particularly suspicious lurking there.

"Now then, Rocky. Time yer were at school, isn't it? Instead of larking about there."

"Oh, cripes!" muttered Rocky. "Call this a free country."

And then the policeman noticed the open front door.

"What yer up to lad? Haven't been breaking in here, have yer?"

"That's right. Go on. Blame me. You think the worst. If there's a brick out of place round here it's that Rocky O'Rourke and the Cats, isn't it?"

Constable McMahon came through into the garden and took hold of Rocky's arm.

"We'll just have a look ... "

"But, listen. It's the old woman. She's not well, see, and I've been looking after her ... "

"We'll just have a look ... "

"I'm telling yer—Billy's gone for help ... Oh, I give up!"

Sullenly Rocky allowed himself to be led back into the house, but when he saw the old woman Constable McMahon changed.

"She needs a doctor. I'll settle with you later, lad. You stay outside while I get an ambulance ... "

"But, I told yer ... "

At the door, however, they met Billy and the wingy, and a few words of explanation settled the matter for the moment. Mr Oliver went in to stay with Mrs Abercrombie while the constable went to phone for an ambulance.

"And you two get off ter school."

"But she didn't want to be taken away," protested

Rocky. "I promised she wouldn't be taken away … "

It was no use. It was all out of Rocky's hands now. As they trudged together through the Square, a crowd was already collecting round Mrs Abercrombie's gate.

"Weren't you on about Mrs Abercrombie the other day?" asked his mother that evening. "Well, they took her away this morning—in an ambulance."

"Hi, Rocky," Beady shouted across the Square later. "They took the mad woman away, and she's got newmonia."

"Rocky—yer know the police have been in ter that house where yer nabbed the transistor," said Nabber.

Rocky shrugged them all off and went to see the wingy. The wingy was standing disconsolately outside the pub in Joseph Terrace.

"Mr Oliver!"

"Hello, Rocky! How are yer?"

"Mr Oliver. What about Mrs Abercrombie?"

"Eh? Oh, the old lady. Well, she's in Sefton Park General. Say she's got pneumonia, and they've sent for her nephew."

"Is she goin' ter die, Mr Oliver?"

"That I don't know, Rocky. How did yer find out she was ill, anyways?"

"Oh—I just noticed she wasn't around." Rocky leaned against the wall, surveying the high barricade of the buildings before him. "She was all right, was Mrs Aber. Mr Oliver, yer know our Joey's gone off."

"I heard that, Rocky. How did the party go?"

"It didn't. He didn't come in for it."

"Well, Rocky, he's a grown man. Got his own life to live. I'll be off meself soon, Rocky."

"Where yer going, Mr Oliver?"

"Looks as though we'll get a flat out at Speke. The

missus doesn't want ter go from here, but. Neither did I. Still, if they don't want me as caretaker, they don't want me."

"Oh, Mr Oliver, don't go! There's Mrs Aber gone, and our Joey gone, and now you!"

"Anyway, Rocky, yer might keep an eye on the old lady's house while it's empty. Yer know what they're like round here once there's nobody in a place."

Rocky nodded gloomily, as though he himself had never ripped out floorboards and window-frames to sell as firewood. "Give them a hammer and there'll only be a gap where the house was in the morning," he agreed. "Wish I was fifteen. I'd clear out of here meself."

There was a sense of uneasiness and of waiting for something to happen in number 3 St Catherine's Square. Not knowing about Joey and what was happening to him made Mrs Flanagan cross, and she shouted at Rocky and Suzie more than ever. It got on Rocky's nerves and he was restless and unhappy.

"What yer going to do about our Joey then?" he asked his mother at last. It was over a week since Joey had come and gone.

"What d'yer mean, what'm I going to do about him? What d'yer think I'm going to do about him?"

"Well yer could do something. Yer could put an advert in the *Echo*."

"And you could mind yer own business!" Standing at the table with a knife in her hand, marging some bread for breakfast, she suddenly moaned, "I've got the intuition again—worse than ever!"

Feeling the old familiar prickle down his spine, Rocky muttered, "She's off again!"

"Just like it was the night yer father left this house for the last time," she went on. "I mind I was standing on the steps and watching him walk down the Square. And I had the intuition. 'He'll not come back again!' I said to meself, and he didn't!"

Mrs Flanagan sighed, spread more marge and dropped the slice of bread before Suzie.

"And last night I had a dream of yer stepfather. Pray God he's not lost to us!"

At this, Suzie stood up, shrieked, and threw her cup at Mrs Flanagan. For a moment, there was silence, then Mrs Flanagan started up, hurling herself at Suzie. Rocky grabbed Suzie and ran with her into the scullery at the back of the house, locking the door behind him.

"Open this door! I'll batter that child. I'll batter the two on youse! She's not right in the head she isn't!"

"What yer do that for, Suzie?" asked Rocky. "Yer crazy!" Hastily considering things, he decided he couldn't leave Suzie to his mother just then. She'd have to go with him. "Look, tatty-'ead, I'm playing footy at Prinney Park and yer'll have to come with me. I'll drop yer through the winder, all right?"

Suzie, unrepentant, nodded, and Rocky hoisted her over the sill and prepared to drop her into the small back-yard outside.

"She shouldn't have said that about my dad," she said, and dropped in a heap on the ground.

"Wait for me," he said and climbed out after her. "We'll give her time to get over it," he said, as they ran through the back lane. "Honest, Suzie, yer more trouble than an army!"

Mr Oliver was with the Cats team that morning, coaching them. Rocky left Suzie to play in the children's play-ground while the team was busy, but his mind wasn't on the game that morning and he missed an easy pass and Mr Oliver called him a plummy.

"What's the matter, lad?" he asked. "What's on yer mind?"

"Well, where's the point in all this then?" demanded Rocky. "Now Chick's Lot's not around, where'll we find a good enough team to play against?"

"Listen ter that will yer! Good enough! You improve yer game and leave me to find the team to play yer!"

"But you're going away."

"Yes, but not this minute. Month's notice yer know. I've got a month's notice after all."

The lake in Princes Park on a fine September day is an ideal place for larking about—or for fishing. Serious fishermen bring tackle and stools, and sit beneath the trees for hours, watching the ducks, and sea birds, the pram-pushing mothers, the dogs and their owners, the boys playing football.

The Cats gang wandered down to the lake after Mr Oliver and the rest of the team had gone home. They fooled around, getting a lot of mud and water on their respective persons.

The sight of Constable McMahon strolling past in the distance on duty did nothing to quieten them, but sent them into dizzy fits of shouting and giggling.

"Hi, there's MacMahon! I bet he comes and chases us. Hi—you with the head on!" Rocky shouted, careful, however, that the constable would not hear.

"Hi, scuffer!"

"Shurrup, Rocky, he's coming!"

And sure enough, the constable had spotted them and was on his way over.

Constable MacMahon stood for several nerve-racking moments in silence behind them. Increasingly nervous, the boys began to fool about again.

"Hi, Rocky, I'll do you. Yer nearly pushed us in!" said the Nabber fiercely.

"Don't get eggy! Hi, me dreams out! Speak of the devil! Can yer smell an awful smell around here?"

"You know like, I think it comes from behind us ... "

"Now, lads, ye'll be in the lake in a minute, and it's deep there. I'm not getting me uniform wet fishing the lot on you out."

"Go on—we can all swim. You know like, little Chan can touch the bottom at the deep end ... "

"What about that brother of yours, Rocky? Is he back?"

"Yes, he is."

"Staying at home, then?"

"No, he's not."

"Pity. I hear he's been hanging about the docks. That'll lead to trouble. Well, lads, keep out of mischief ... "

The constable went on his way.

Rocky spat.

"He's the one nabbed our Joey. Him and the 'tec—what's his name? You know like, 'tective Hounslow. They wus tipped off else they'd never 'ave got on to our kid."

"Yer mean he was snitched on?" asked Beady.

"Wouldn't have got him else."

The Nabber laughed scornfully.

"I'll bet!"

"What d'yer mean?"

"Anybody could get on ter your kid. He was that daft! Couldn't take a rattle from a baby!"

"Hi, that'll do you! Our kid's the best in this town—I'm telling yer! You know nowt about it. Yer talk like a half-penny book, you do!"

"Who does?"

"You do."

"Say that again!"

The Nabber squared up for a fight. Rocky straightened his shoulders scornfully.

"You couldn't punch a hole in a wet newspaper!"

"Hi, listen, Rocky," broke in Beady, "who snitched on your kid, then?"

"It was Jimmy Simpson—the big boss. He's dead rich."

"How d'*you* know?" interjected the Nabber.

"Listen, Nabber, that'll do you or I'll put yer eye in a sling!"

"All right, all right. Yer needn't shout."

"Well you mind yer lip!"

A certain gloom settled over the gang at the end of this argument. It seemed as though Joey's return had cast a blight over their activities. Trying to dispel it, Rocky explained that he intended, the following evening, to go down to the docks and find a warehouse for the big break-in. The Nabber was enthusiastic, but had his doubts.

"Yer can count me in—all right," he said, "but how yer going ter do it? How yer going to choose the right place?"

"What d'yer mean?"

"Well, it all depends what's in the place, doesn't it? I mean, suppose it's full of—of washing machines—what's the good of breaking in ter that? Yer couldn't get them away. See Chick's Lot was clever—they did flats and houses, yer can choose the right loot, that way."

"They weren't so clever that they didn't get caught," said Billy.

"Course they weren't," said Rocky. "They shouldn't have pinched from near their own doorsteps." Rocky had a strong feeling now against going into someone's house again and stealing. It no longer seemed right to him. A

91

house belonged to somebody—a warehouse, so far as he was concerned, belonged to nobody.

"Yes, an' warehouses got people guarding them—and dogs! Do you know what those can do? Do you know what they train them to do? I saw a picture on telly ... " began Nabber, becoming enthusiastic.

"I'll have ter go," said Billy suddenly. The Cats weren't the gang he wanted to be in if they were off on that lark again.

"I also must go," said little Chan, who felt as Billy did.

"What time is it? I'll have ter go as well." The Nabber, Beady and Chan began walking in the direction of the gates that opened on to the Boulevard. Billy lingered a moment.

"Yer coming, Rocky?"

"No. I'll hang around a bit. Hi, Billy, when yer pass the kids' playground tell tatty-'ead to come ... "

Rocky went and sat in the shelter that overlooked the lake. It wasn't warm, but at least it was out of the cold wind. Suzie soon joined him, and they sat together with red noses and chill fingers and stared out over the park.

Rocky's thoughts were troubled. Joey had always said he'd get Jim Simpson when he came out, for framing him. But it didn't look that way now. It looked as if Joey was keeping out of his way.

For the first time Rocky began to have doubts. Maybe Joey wasn't as clever as he said. Maybe he wasn't up to taking on Jim Simpson. Maybe that was why he hadn't come home, because he didn't want Jim Simpson to find him.

"That's daft!" he exclaimed, pulling himself up. Joey wasn't scared. And as for Chick—well, Chick hadn't Joey's brains. He was bound to get caught.

"There was a big lad pushed me off the slide," commented Suzie.

"Uh?" said Rocky absent-mindedly, his thoughts returning to Billy and little Chan. They were chicken, he decided. Chicken.

"I battered him," said Suzie with satisfaction.

Rocky shivered. He felt that *he'd* got the intuition now, just like his mother. Something was going to happen. Got the intuition worse than the toothache, he thought.

"I'm hungry," said Suzie.

"Oh all right, tatty-'ead. Come on!"

CHAPTER
11

BUT once again, Mrs Flanagan's intuition had been right. That day she had had a letter from Rocky's step-father.

"He'll be home this week. There now. I knew he wouldn't be long. We'll see if he can't find our Joey—and you keep yerself out of mischief, lad, or he'll give you a battering as well!"

Rocky had sneered, red hair scornfully on end, and he'd gone out straight away, wandering down to the end of the Square where, from St James's Mount, he could look down over the town and the docks to where the river bristled with cranes and masts and funnels. The dusky mist of the September evening was smudging out the streets under the smoky red of the western sky. The cathedral towered up into it. The old houses of the Square were dilapidated sentinels of past years, and looming over them was the new block of flats, its lights gradually coming on, standing up like a big liner. He could see the lights down on the river, the lights from the Cheshire bank, and he could hear the sallow hoot of a boat from the river.

It was from the river that his father had sailed, and arrived back with presents from over the world. And it was from that river his father had sailed on his last voyage.

Now his stepfather would come from the same river, but for Rocky he was an intruder, claiming a relationship with him that didn't exist.

He remembered having an argument once with Betty

Mulloney across the road. "You can get another da, but you can never get another mam," she had said, with an air of pious virtue.

"Well," Rocky had retorted, pointing to Suzie, "*she* did. *She* got another mam."

"Yes, but not her real mam."

"No—no more'n he's my real dad."

"Soon as I can," Rocky thought, "I'll go to sea. I'll get a job on a ship. I'll get away."

Meanwhile, he was like a rudderless speed-boat, rushing and tearing haphazard about the sea of streets.

"You should be pleased. Yer dad's coming back," he said to Suzie, who had followed him out. Suzie didn't answer. She was gazing also down at the river and the lights. And Rocky knew that her father's second marriage upset her as much as his mother's second marriage upset him.

"You know like, Suzie, you won't go off again, will yer? Before he comes back, I mean?"

Suzie said nothing, skipping on and off the edge of the pavement.

"Go on then, tatty-'ead. You'd better get in."

There'd been someone in Mrs Abercrombie's, and the front door had been open. Rocky had dashed over hoping to find she was back, but instead he'd found a youngish man standing in the garden ruefully surveying the weeds, and the two broken windows the house already boasted.

"You want something?"

"I just wondered if Mrs Aber was back, mister."

"Mrs Who?"

"Mrs Abercrombie—you know, she went into hospital with newmonia."

"She's not coming back."

"Is she not better?"

"Oh, she's coming round. But when she's better she's coming to live with me. I'm her nephew. You live round here?"

"Number 3."

"Any idea who's been breaking these windows?"

"Yer can't trust anybody round here, mister. Yer can't leave a place empty two minutes. They'll take it apart. Mind, it wasn't my lot done this—they wouldn't harm Mrs Aber's house. My lot's the Cats gang, and I'm Rocky O'Rourke."

"So you're Rocky?" The man looked at him with more interest. "My aunt's been talking about you. Says you saved her life. She says she'll be writing you a letter and asking you to come and stay with us some time. We live in the country, you know. Beyond Chester."

"Hi, that'll be smashin'. Can I bring Suzie? She's never been in the country."

"I expect so ..."

"Are yer selling the house?"

"Well, I thought I'd break it into flats ... Thing is, somebody should be around to look after it."

"You know like, yer need a caretaker. I know one—he'd come if I asked him. He's a smashing caretaker. He caretakes all the Buildings—the whole lot of them."

"He wouldn't want to leave a job like that then."

"Yes he would." Rocky thought fast. "It's too much for him, yer see—all the stairs. Shall I tell him? His name's Mr Oliver ..."

"Hm? I'll think about it."

But Rocky went haring off to tell Mr Oliver immediately.

"I put a good word in for yer," he said. "You should go and see him. Go on, Mr Oliver."

Mr Oliver looked thoughtful, then he said, "All right,

96

Rocky. I will."

It was with some feeling of satisfaction that Rocky went to the youth club again a few days after. At least the wingy mightn't be going away, and maybe his stepfather wouldn't stay too long, and maybe Joey would come back. He splashed through a wet night towards the Baptist hall, whistling. But his luck was out, because that was the night they threw him out of the youth club. Somehow or other everything got his back up that night.

To begin with, they asked about Joey, and he had to make things up to save his face. And then they had to comment about his footwear.

"Rocky—you're wet through. Have you no stronger shoes than those?"

It was one of the helpers at the club—the woman helper. Rocky scowled furiously. He resented interference in his own personal concerns from anyone—even his mother. And he hated having to admit that he possessed nothing but the Jesus-boots.

"What's the matter with them? They're all right. Anyway, they're my feet in them, aren't they?"

"Now, Rocky, there's no need to be cheeky."

"He's always cheeky. He's the cheekiest one in the Square." It was Betty Mulloney. Always pushing her nose into things.

"Shurrup dur! Mind yer own business or I'll bash yer when yer get outside."

"Rocky—we'll have no talk like that here … "

"He shouldn't be here anyway," Betty Mulloney went on, undaunted. "Mr Cooper said last year he hadn't to come back. He only comes for the Christmas party, then he stops!"

Not even the fiery gleams from Rocky's eyes stopped

this flow. Betty Mulloney said her piece and flounced away virtuously.

"That's a lie—honest, miss, she's a liar ... "

"I hope it's not true, anyway, Rocky. Now come along, we're having bingo ... "

Bingo! Rocky hated it. Sitting there putting soppy discs on soppy cards. He was furious. With everything, and especially with the youth club. His anger erupted gradually into shouting 'house' when he hadn't got one, upsetting his neighbour's card, and picking a fight with the boy behind him. Before being told to leave, he created havoc in the quiet room, and had a fight over paying his subs. It wasn't his night, and he knew his dismissal from the club was coming—and it came. That meant no party for him or Suzie.

Standing on the steps of the church hall, Rocky shouted a few threats at the closed door and, hunching his shoulders, he set out in the rain.

It was as he was entering the Square that the big grey Jaguar drew up silently beside him, and Jim Simpson's head appeared at the window.

Rocky's blood froze. He must be looking for Joey. His mind flashed back to the time he'd seen Jim Simpson trailing Joey in that car.

"Hi, you, little 'un!" called Jim Simpson to Rocky. "You're Joey O'Rourke's brother, aren't you? Didn't I see you at Pier Head?"

Now Rocky was small for his age, but he objected to anything being made of it, and his red hair bristled with indignation, fear forgotten.

"What if I am?"

"Where is he?"

"How should I know, wack?"

"He's back isn't he?"

"I wudden know!"

Jim Simpson was nonplussed. He looked round at the rows of huge, grimy old houses, as though expecting to see Joey at the window of one of them.

Rock stood stockily staring at him, his hair flaming, his yellow eyes narrowed with antagonism.

"Well, yer can give him a message when yer see him, titch," Jim Simpson continued. "Tell him Jim Simpson's out ter get him. All right?"

"Tell him yerself, wack. I'm not yer servant."

Jim Simpson suddenly realized that Rocky was being offensive and turned his attention on him.

"Hey, kid. Keep a civil tongue in yer head, or yer'll go the same way as him. Just you tell him—Jim Simpson's out ter get him!"

The Jaguar moved off, and Rocky, filled with rage, made various vulgar gestures after it, dancing off the pavement and shouting,

"Gerron! Yer cudden do our kid! Takes a man norra shirt button! Gerron!"

"Hi, Rocky!"

The Cats came belting towards him, Billy pedalling fast on his tricycle alongside them.

"Hi, Rocky!" The Nabber was in the lead. "Was that Jim Simpson? Hi, what's he want?"

"He was after Joey."

"Hi, Rocky, yer didn't half tell him where to get off!" said the Nabber, and the Cats felt real admiration for their leader who wasn't afraid to face up to a man like Simpson.

"He's not pushing the O'Rourkes around," said Rocky. The gang went to shelter in the archway leading to the flats, standing in a group with their shoulders hunched against the cold and watching the rain falling.

"I'm going down the docks to find Joey," said Rocky

coming to a decision. "I've got to let him know about Jim Simpson, see." Suddenly Rocky hissed, "Shurrup! The scuffer," and they fell silent, crouching in the shadows as they heard the constable's regular, heavy footfall on the pavement beyond. The footsteps stopped and the Cats waited, listening.

A lighter, quicker step was heard, and then a voice.

"Hello, dur! Constable McMahon, isn't it?"

Rocky's heart leapt.

"Me stepfather!" he muttered. "He's back already!"

"Mr Flanagan! Just back, are yer?"

"On me way home. And glad to be back, as well."

"Well, I'm glad ter see yer. They could do with yer around."

"Not trouble, is there?"

"Yer know Joey was back?"

"I didn't."

"He's come and gone again. From what I heard, he paid a visit home and cleared off down to the docks. And the company he's keeping's not all that good."

"I'm sorry ter hear that. But I never could get through to Joey. He has it in for me, yer know. He wanted me ter give him an alibi for that night he did the job—I wouldn't do it. But Joey doesn't see these things very straight ... "

The two men began to move on down the street, and their voices faded.

Rocky was shocked. He'd never been told that before. He'd never realized just how much Flanagan had let Joey down.

"Are yer going home, Rocky?" asked Billy.

"I am not. Not with him there! So he wouldn't help Joey! I didn't know that. Come on, Nabber. Are yer coming ter have a look round the docks for Joey?"

Without pausing for an answer, Rocky started down the street towards the river, his shoulders slouched, hands in his pockets.

"I'm going home," said Billy.

"See yer then, Billy," said the Nabber, and slouched after Rocky.

Beady and little Chan hesitated, then Beady ran after them, and little Chan said to Billy, "I walk round home with you, Billy."

"O.K. See yer, Rocky!" shouted Billy, turning his bicycle and pedalling reluctantly home.

"See yer!" came Rocky's voice from the distance.

CHAPTER
12

ROCKY had no idea where he was going or what he was going to do, but it gave him a sense of relief to be skulking and plunging through the dark streets towards the dock, bent on finding Joey and warning him.

"Tell yer what," he said, "when we're down we'll have a look round. See if we can find a warehouse to do at the same time, eh?"

The other two were in agreement, but the docks in Liverpool were built many years ago with a view to keeping trespassers and thieves out. The warehouses along the dock road presented a solid barrier of heavy stone to would-be entrants.

Rocky and the others slouched along in the shadows, becoming more and more frustrated. Not a gate that was climbable, not a window, not a break anywhere.

"Ah, come on, Rocky, I'm fed up wi' this. I'm going home," said Beady, at last.

"We'll look around tomorrer—it'll be easier to find him," said the Nabber.

"Please yerselves. I'm going on," said Rocky, and tucking his hands in his anorak to warm them, he strode on through the darkness.

"He's nuts!" exclaimed the Nabber. "Yer nuts, Rocky!" he shouted.

"Hi, Rocky! Come on," shouted Beady.

"Hi, Rocky!"

Rocky turned a corner and found himself right in the middle of a group of young men, lounging in the darkness, some with motor bikes.

"All right, little 'un, where yer off to?"

"It's Rocky, in'it? I heard them shouting of yer, our kid."

"Joey! Hi, Joey, what yer doing here?"

"What *you* doin' here, wack? And who's this with yer?"

Beady and the Nabber had come pelting round after him.

"Who are they?" asked somebody.

"My kid brother. What yer up to, Rocky?"

In the face of this adult gang, Rocky rose to occasion. "We was looking a job over," he said airily. "What was youse doing?"

To his annoyance, his comment only aroused hoots and laughter from the others.

"Did yer get that? Looking a job over!"

"Which one did yer have in mind?"

"Can we join yer gang, then? Big stuff this, in'it!"

Rocky scowled, and put up his fists.

"All right, then. Come on," he threatened, "which on yer's coming first?"

"Hi, wack, he scares me!"

"He's a fighter, in't he?"

"Let him alone," said Joey. "Come on, Rocky, come on, I'll walk yer home some of the way. I've got a deal for yer. Yer pals can come as well."

They walked back towards St James's Mount, Joey trundling his bike along the pavement's edge.

"Yer know the scuffers after yer, our kid," said Rocky. "McMahon was asking about yer, and Jimmy Simpson … "

"They've got nothin' on me."

"You know, Joey, Flanagan's back."

"Is he? Has he got any money?"

"Don't know. Haven't seen him yet."

"I'll have to pay him a visit. He'll be missing me!" said Joey sarcastically. "Want to do a job for me, Rocky?"

"What kinder job?"

"Easy, and there'll be money in it for yer. Next Thursday night … "

"What about these two?"

"They're in on it."

"All right, lads?" asked Rocky.

"All right, Rocky," they replied.

They gathered round Joey.

"It's easy," he repeated. "Next Thursday, about five. You go down to the dockside, and there'll be a ship in— the *Rosemary*. Now yer'll find a bloke there on duty. All yer got to do is shout to him, 'Hi mister, let's have a look over yer ship.' Got it?"

"Yes."

"Then he'll say come on then, and ter go aboard. When he's showing yer round, he'll slip yer a packet. Small thing, but yer'd better have something to put it in … "

"Me fishing basket … " said Rocky.

"Right. Then yer get off the ship, and go along to the landing stage—I'll be there with me bike, but I'll wait in the snack bar, see. Come in there, I'll buy youse a coffee, and when yer can, slip me the parcel. All right?"

"All right, wack! What is it, our kid? Is it something big?"

"Big enough, Rocky. Now mind yer don't let me down … See yer!"

Rocky stood still, his blood racing with excitement.

"See, I told yer we'd get in with our kid," he proclaimed. "I told yer! Told yer he'd take us on. This is not kid's stuff now, is it?"

On the way home, they passed the Baptist hall, its lights blazing and sounds of singing coming from it as the choir were practising.

"They put me out of the youth club," Rocky said. "They put me out because ... Here!" He had a sudden idea for getting his own back. In a few moments, the three of them had climbed up on to the roof of the hall. They marched up and down until the choir members came rushing out in protest.

Rocky, the Nabber and Beady jumped down again and ran off along the dark streets hooting with laughter. It had been a good night.

CHAPTER
13

It was very late by the time they reached the Square again, but there was still a light in number 3.

"What's up now?" said Rocky. "Me mam's sitting up."

He burst in to the kitchen and then stopped suddenly as his mother and stepfather turned rather anxiously to him.

"So yer back at last. And where d'yer think yer've been till this time?" shouted his mother. "And yer stepfather waiting ter see yer."

"Hello, Rocky, lad! How are yer?"

"All right."

Rocky sat down sullenly, trying to control the antagonism he felt towards this man.

"That's no way to speak ter yer stepfather!" and Mrs Flanagan landed him one.

"Let him be," said Mr Flanagan. "Give the lad time. Ye're late, Rocky."

"Been with the lads."

"Want some supper?"

"I had some chips."

Rocky felt aggrieved and angry. His mother always sided with Flanagan against him. The stale, oppressive atmosphere of home grew round him.

"I'm going ter bed … "

Rocky went into the other room where he was to sleep with Suzie now. Suzie was curled up in bed, a Japanese doll that her father had brought her on the pillow beside her.

She was smiling in her sleep.

Rocky took off his trousers and jumper and sandals and crept into his own bed, pulling an old coat over him for warmth.

Shivering, he thought of the job he would do on Thursday with Joey. That would be exciting. Better than being at home with Flanagan there.

And in the living-room, Mr Flanagan sat back in his chair and looked thoughtfully into the glow of the fire.

"I can do nothing with him," his wife was saying. "Yer see how it is. He'll go the way of our Joey!"

Mr Flanagan shook his head. "No he won't. Not if I can help it!"

For the next few days, Rocky found it wasn't so easy to get out by himself just by saying he was "going out". The question always came from his stepfather, "Where to?" So he didn't sag school, and in the evening his stepfather took him and Suzie out. Once he took them down to the docks, and once to the merchant navy club to see his pals. Another time they went to the pictures and had ice creams in the interval and fish and chips afterwards from Chan's. And Rocky had to admit Mr Flanagan wasn't a bad sort. He could tell them lots of stories about foreign places, so that pretty soon you began to expect that when you went out of number 3, you would find yourself in the streets of Calcutta, or at Sydney harbour.

But Rocky didn't let it make him forget about Thursday, and even if he didn't see the gang so much, it was just as well, he told himself. Keep out of trouble until the night!

Wednesday night, he met the wingy outside the pub. Mr Oliver had good news.

"Yer got the job, Mr Oliver?"

"I did. Me wife and me's ter have the basement flat, and

I'll be working over there just now helping to get the place cleaned out. The wife's pleased, I can tell yer, Rocky. We didn't want ter move out of this area ... "

"I'm that glad, Mr Oliver!"

His father was waiting for him when he got home.

"Want some supper, Rocky?"

"I had some chips."

"Rocky, when d'yer leave school?"

"Two years time I'll be fifteen."

"What'll yer do then?"

Rocky shrugged. "I haven't thought. The Nabber says he'll get a job down the docks. Maybe I'll go with him. The Nabber's father'll fix it."

"What about coming to sea—with me? Would yer not like ter see all them foreign parts?"

Rocky hesitated. It was a good idea—and it attracted him. It would be something, that would.

"I don't know. Mebbe."

"Think about it, Rocky."

"Right. I will."

"And Rocky—what about coming ter see the wrestling tomorrer night?"

This time Rocky did hesitate—and with regret.

"Can't—I've—I've got something on ... "

"All right, Rocky. We'll go another time."

Rocky went to bed, thoughtfully. He would have liked the wrestling—still it was nothing to doing a job with Joey!

The waters of the Mersey were grey and restless, the cold wind up from the sea pressed about the three boys, looking for the *Rosemary*. Lights were already springing up along the streets, and on the ships at anchor in the grey chill of the river. The dockers were streaming out of the gates, lorries were churning along the streets near the docks.

"Hi, good time for doing some lorry-skipping," shouted the Nabber.

They were all hilarious with excitement.

"Shurrup—we've gotta bunk in here … "

It wasn't so difficult for the three boys to squeeze in through the crowds coming out of the docks, without being noticed. It might be difficult getting out again with the package, but they would face that later.

They dodged along the quayside, avoiding notice as much as possible, and finally found the *Rosemary*, a much smaller ship than they imagined, her decks completely deserted.

"This is it," said Rocky. "Where's the feller?"

"We'll have ter shout for him."

Rocky stood back, looking up the gang-plank, and shouted,

"Hi, mister!"

There was no response.

"Hi, mister … mister! Hi! … " their voices rose and scattered on the autumn wind.

There was a moment of blank, baffled silence. A ship, moving up-river beyond, hooted.

The boys shuddered.

"It's cold enough fur two pairs of bootlaces," said Rocky.

"What'll we do, Rocky?" asked Beady.

"We'll have ter go on to her," said Rocky.

"Is it all right?"

But Rocky was already on the gang-plank. The other two followed, more warily.

On deck, light streamed from the windows of the deck-house.

"Watch yer noise," warned Rocky, and cautiously approached the porthole. He peered in.

The other two heard him gasp and crept over to look. Inside the cabin a man in sailor's uniform was backed up against the wall. He was looking both surly and terrified. A parcel done up in brown paper lay on a table, and standing over the man, threateningly, was a big thug. Seated beside the table was Jim Simpson.

The porthole was slightly open, and Rocky put his ear to it.

" ... wasn't handing it over, see ... " the seaman was saying.

"No? Then why've yer been around with Joey O'Rourke if yer weren't double-crossing us? And why wasn't this handed over straight off?" asked Jim Simpson touching the parcel.

"I'm trying to tell yer ... I couldn't get away tonight ... "

"Where's Joey O'Rourke now? Is he coming here?"

"I don't know anythink about Joey O'Rourke ... "

"Persuade him," said Jim Simpson, and the thug raised his fist.

Rocky gave an involuntary exclamation as the seaman flinched back, and Jim Simpson looked up suddenly. For a moment, Rocky and he stared at each other, then Jim Simpson moved quickly, and Rocky cried,

"Gerrout—he's seen us!"

The boys clattered along the deck towards the gangplank. Behind them, the cabin door was flung open, and footsteps came after them.

Terrified now, the whole thing no longer an exciting game, the boys fled along the shadows of the docks towards the nearest gate. The gates were closed, all but a small inset door, and they threw themselves out through it to the protests of the guards.

Beside the pavement, a grey Jaguar stood menacingly.

"Come on!" Rocky hurled himself across the road, his mind sufficiently calm to choose the narrowest and darkest streets and lanes up the slope of St James's Mount. At the churchyard they paused, panting and listening. There was no sound of anything following.

"We've got rid of them," said Rocky.

"But he recognized yer," said the Nabber.

"Yes. He'll be after our kid." Rocky thought desperately. He couldn't leave Joey in ignorance. He might go to the docks seeking them, and fall straight into a trap.

"Youse go home. I'm going to tell Joey."

The snack bar at the landing stage was crowded and hot. It took a while for Rocky to find his brother leaning against the counter, looking round anxiously.

Rocky slipped up to him.

"Rocky! Yer got it?"

"No—Jim Simpson was there—he was on the boat."

A look of fear passed over Joey's face.

"Yer sure?"

"He was in the cabin talking to the feller, and he had the parcel. He saw me, and he chased us."

"Is he follering yer?"

Rocky shook his head.

"No, Joey—I shook him off ... Will yer go and do him, Joey?"

"Look, wack, you keep out of his way—and mine!"

Joey began pushing towards the door.

"But, Joey!"

"I told yer!"

Rocky fell back among the crowds and Joey vanished. He couldn't understand it—not any of it.

CHAPTER
14

IT was Billy who, a day or so later, came limping down to the hideout where the Cats were assembled, with a copy of the *Liverpool Echo*.

"Here—seen this, Rocky?"

The front page carried a report of the finding of a body in the Mersey, identified as that of the mate of the *Rosemary*, a small cargo ship trading between Liverpool and the Far East, and currently in the Mersey. The man was thought to have been killed two days before. It was also thought that he was involved with a gang smuggling heroin into the country.

"Is that him? The mate on the *Rosemary*?" asked Billy breathlessly.

Rocky and Nabber had told the gang the story of the *Rosemary* over and over again, and they wondered what it had all been about, and what was in the parcel they were supposed to collect.

Rocky nodded. "It's him, isn't it, Nabber?"

"Who killed him, d'yer think?"

"Must have been that feller with Jim Simpson."

Billy became very earnest.

"Look, Rocky, you'll have to tell the police."

"Go on—and get meself and Joey in trouble?"

"I bet Jim Simpson's after your Joey now," Nabber said.

"After our Joey? Yer codding! Our Joey'll be after him." But in spite of his brave words Rocky was puzzled, and he had a gnawing doubt about Joey. Why had he been afraid of Jim Simpson? He hadn't been codding Rocky all this time, had he?

"But Rocky, don't yer see?" said Billy. "It's you's in danger—you can prove Simpson was mixed up in this smuggling gang, and in the murder. You'd be a witness. If he can get rid of yer, he will!"

"He's right," said Beady.

"Mebbe," said Rocky, "but I'm not frightened of Jim Simpson. And I'm not going to the scuffers."

Rocky could not be persuaded, and Billy gave up at last, but he was very troubled, and the Nabber and Beady decided that, for a few days, they should all stay at home as much as possible.

The next evening, Suzie was late in for tea and Mrs Flanagan got into a flap immediately.

"Go and find her, Rocky," she said anxiously. "For goodness sake bring her home before Flanagan finds she's gone. He'll blame me, sure thing!"

Rocky hurried off on the search, but to his surprise he soon found her, running along the cold, lamp-lit street towards him.

"Hi, tatty-'ead, where yer been?" he greeted. "Come on, yer mam's in a state."

Suzie said nothing. She put her cold hand into his, and allowed herself to be taken home. Mrs Flanagan scolded, but Rocky only took Suzie to her bedroom, pulled off her jumper and jeans, and got her into bed.

"All right, tatty-'ead?" he asked.

Suzie's dirty face looked back at him from over the ragged blanket.

"Where yer been, anyway? And what d'yer do it for, Suzie?"

"I got a note for yer," she said unexpectedly.

"A note?"

"In me jeans. He gave it to me."

"Who? What yer on about?"

Rocky picked up her jeans and felt in the pocket. Sure enough, there was a small crumpled note. A piece torn out of a diary with some words written on it in pencil:

"Need help. Very dangerous."

It was signed "Joey".

"Where d'yer get this, Suzie?" Rocky demanded.

"A man give it ter me."

"But where, Suzie? Where was he?"

Suzie's eyes were drooping with sleep. "Down there," she murmured.

Down there? Where did she mean?

"The cemetery!"

She must mean St James's. Rocky stood thinking. If Joey was there, he was hiding from somebody—maybe the scuffers, maybe Simpson's gang. He'd have to go to Joey's help, but he'd have to go carefully, in case they were watching out.

Rocky pulled on his anorak and tiptoed out down the passage towards the door. No point in telling his mother he was going out. She'd only create.

He couldn't see how he was going to get into the cemetery—he couldn't squeeze between the railings like Suzie. He went to the front of the cathedral, carefully looking round to make sure he wasn't followed, then he dodged from the lighted street and into the shadows beneath the tower. He ran, his footsteps echoing loudly against the great walls. The gate into the cemetery was locked, but he had to get through. It wasn't easy to climb it, but with a struggle—and a torn sleeve—he reached the top, hung by his hands for a moment, and then dropped into the bushes on the other side.

Panting and not a little nervous, he stood up cautiously and looked down on the great valley of graves. Lights from the streets round about lit up a tree-top here and shone upon a stone monument there, but mostly it was shadowed and still and silent. Not a movement. Not a sound. Only the occasional roar of a car on the streets beyond, an isolated shout from some alley.

How was he to find Joey here? But surely he would be expecting him and on the lookout? Bracing himself, Rocky plunged down the steep slope towards the graves.

For some time he crept cautiously along one path after another, looking for his brother wherever a larger monument than usual might give him shelter. Suddenly, a shadow moved, a voice said hoarsely, "Rocky!"

It was Joey.

Joey lay propped against the steps of a large monument of columns with a roof. He didn't get up.

"Joey—what's the matter? Are yer all right?"

"Did they see yer coming?"

"Nobody saw me—who's after yer?"

"Jim Simpson's gang. They caught me and beat me up, but I got away. They'll kill me if they catch me again … It's so cold … "

"Yer can't stay here, Joey," said Rocky. "Yer'll have to come home with me … "

"Can't. They'll be watching the house. So will the scuffers. It's over a job I done … "

Rocky sank down against a pillar. It was damp and chill and silent there, and the great cathedral loomed above, like an unconcerned and giant sentinel. Rocky was shocked and upset by the change in his brother. The confident, swaggering Joey was gone, and in his place was a shivering, frightened fugitive.

"I have to get away, Rocky. Yer've got to help me. I've got it worked out. There's a feller with a boat—he'll be down near the landing stage tomorrow. He's called Durr—Hans Durr. Can yer remember that? Yer'll have to see him. Tell him I'll be sailing with him tomorrow. He promised me he'd take me. He'll drop me off somewhere in Scotland, then I'll be all right. Yer got it, Rocky?"

"But—what's he look like?"

"Can't miss him—bald, he is, and red-faced. Dresses like a tramp. Always sitting in the snack bar down on the lanny. Yer can't miss him ... "

"The lush? Yer mean the ... "

"Yes, but he's all right. He'll get me out. Now listen, mind yer not followed, Rocky, and get back ter me with the message, skin. Yer will, won't yer?"

He shivered with the cold.

"Got anything on yer to eat?"

Rocky thought for a moment.

"I could douse on Simpson for yer," he said.

"What d'yer mean?"

"I saw him in—in the cabin, with the mate of the *Rosemary*. I could tell the scuffers ... "

"Keep away from him, skin. Yer can't fight Simpson. Keep out of his way ... "

Rain began falling, and Joey shuddered.

"Yer can't stay here," said Rocky. "Yer'll freeze. Listen, our kid, I've got a hideout ... "

"I'm not risking it ... "

"It's safe. Nobody'll find yer. Come on, I'll get yer to it tonight, and I'll see this feller tomorrer ... "

Rocky never thought that he would be guiding Joey, telling him what to do. But Joey was changed. Joey was frightened and on the run.

Cautiously, Rocky going ahead, they climbed out of the

graveyard, and Rocky led the way through dark and deserted alleys to the gang hideout. He lit a candle, and Joey dropped on to the old settee. His clothes were torn and dirty, there was a bruise on his forehead, and his lip was cut.

"Put the light out … !"

"It's all right. The windows is boarded."

There were some Oxo cubes left, and Rocky boiled the kettle and made Joey a cup. He drank it thankfully, and Rocky found a packet of biscuits for him.

"I'll bring some food tomorrow—and some clothes," he said as he was going.

"Rocky … remember. Watch out for Simpson. If he finds me I'm done for … "

Rocky nodded, and crept out again into the silent midnight streets.

CHAPTER
15

His mother and stepfather and Suzie were asleep. Rocky took off his jumper and trousers and crept thankfully under the blankets, but not to sleep. He couldn't stop thinking about Joey, Joey the big leader who was now shivering and frightened in the hideout. Rocky's dreams about his brother had been finally shattered that night, all his half-doubts confirmed. Joey had never been brave, he saw that now. Joey had been a small-time crook, and Joey had been caught. Like Chick. And Rocky didn't want to end up that way. He didn't want to end up on the run from the police. He wanted to do something better than that.

But even though he no longer admired Joey, he couldn't let him down now. Something had to be done.

He could go to Constable McMahon tomorrow and tell him what he'd seen on the *Rosemary*. Then they'd pick up Jim Simpson. But that wouldn't help Joey. Joey said the scuffers were after him as well.

He slept at last, but he was awake again at seven, and up at the window looking out on to the square for the sight of somebody lurking about, or the big grey Jag. There were some workmen starting off for work—a motor bike was being revved up, a man on a bicycle came from the archway to the flats. That was all.

Rocky had a hasty wash at the sink and pulled on his trousers, jumper and anorak. He took tea, sugar and a tin of milk, made up some butties, helped himself to some eggs and biscuits, and a cold pie. That left very little in the larder but it couldn't be helped.

He opened the front door cautiously and slipped out into the chill morning air. The river valley was filled with a misty haze—only the cathedral tower rose above it into the grey sky.

Joey had been sleeping, and was obviously terrified by his knock, but he took the food greedily, and Rocky made tea. They sat drinking it.

"It's cold!" Joey said. "I'll be glad to get out of here—glad to get away for good."

"Where'll yer go, Joey?"

"Don't know yet. But I'll get away somewhere—abroad. Did yer bring some money?"

"I haven't got much ... "

"I mean real money—I'll need a few pounds."

"But ... "

"Me mam has some—she'll keep it in her purse. Yer can bring it after yer've seen Hans Durr. But don't tell her ... she'll only create."

"I'm not stealing off our mam."

"Why not? She'd give it if she knew ... "

"I know but ... "

"I've got ter have it, skin."

Rocky stood stockily, his feet apart, his red hair bristling, his yellow eyes determined.

"I'm not stealing off our mam."

"Oh all right." Joey stood sulkily brooding. "Look, I'll need some of me things from home."

"I'll pack them up and drop them down the area if I can. Yer'd better stay in here till dark. I wouldn't come out because Jim Simpson's been around here once or twice and he might be around again."

"Yer won't forget to tell Durr? Tell him I'm definitely coming, see, and he has to wait for me. I'll nip out soon as it's dark ... "

"All right, our kid." Rocky thought things out. "I'll sag school and go down and see Durr now. If I can come back ter see yer I will. All right?"

Joey promised to drop a postcard to Rocky as soon as he was safe somewhere, and Rocky started back home. He wouldn't feel Joey was really safe until next morning when the tide had turned and the boat left. And as for himself—when would he feel safe, knowing Jim Simpson was about?

The Square was clear, Rocky raced across it, but as he was passing Mrs Abercrombie's, he saw a grey Jaguar turning into the Square. Rocky leapt into the garden, panting.

"Hello, Rocky, lad. Up early, aren't yer?"

It was the wingy, smoking a morning pipe. The door was open, and through the passage he could see Mrs Oliver in a large overall, cleaning the house.

"Hello, Mr Oliver."

"You look worried, Rocky. What's up?"

"Nothing. Yer moved in here now, Mr Oliver?"

"Not yet. Me and the wife's cleaning it out. They're coming to move the furniture out tomorrow, then the builders'll be in to do some alterations." Mr Oliver, who had been watching the Square through the screen of the hedge, moved forward. "You know, Rocky, in this garden, it's so shut in and peaceful, yer would think yer were in the country. Just a second, son. There's a car going round and round out there—mebbe's looking for somebody ... "

"No, mister! Don't go!" Rocky exclaimed.

The wingy turned round.

"You in trouble?"

Rocky frowned. He needed help, but he couldn't scat on Joey.

"Look, Rocky, if it's real trouble, don't play about, lad. I know the coppers well—I can soon have a word with them."

"I know it's real, all right, Mr Oliver, but I'm not scatting—not to the scuffers. I—I can't. See, it's not just me in trouble ... "

The lorry-skipping, and getting into Mrs Abercrombie's, that had just been for the excitement—to make yer sweat. But he was sweating now in good earnest. It wasn't a game any longer with that car out there moving round the square, nosing him out.

"Well, if it's any help, Rocky, that Jag's just gone out on to Catherine Street."

"Thanks—I'll be off, then."

"Here, Rocky—yer'll mebbe need a bob or two ... "

"Thanks, Mr Oliver!"

Rocky peered out of the garden. It seemed clear. Clutching the two shilling piece, he raced across to number 3 like a rabbit.

The family was up. A breakfast of cereals was being eaten—an unusual thing, and his stepfather's innovation.

"Why, Rocky! Out already?"

"Aye—I had ter see ter something."

"Come an' get yer breakfast. Yer'll be late for school."

As naturally as he could, Rocky ate some breakfast, then sneaked into the other room. In the cupboard there were some of Joey's things. He stuffed them, haphazard, into an old pillow case, and started for the door.

"Rocky—you come back! I've some messages for yer to get on yer way back from school!" shouted his mother, but Rocky ignored her. At the door, Ellen-from-upstairs was putting out the baby in his pram. She looked up at Rocky through her long hair.

"In a hurry the day, Rocky?"

Rocky did not reply. He shot across the Square, dropped the bundle down the area of the old vicarage, and leapt down the Steps. He hared along past the shops, tore up Upper Parliament Street, and arrived panting at the bus stop.

There was a bus coming. He could see it along Prince's Boulevard. But in front of it was a car—the grey Jag. They were after him. Sure to see him standing there. But it didn't matter, if he could only get on to the bus.

The Jaguar passed him, and stopped a few yards beyond. Rocky saw Jim Simpson looking back at him, then he started to get out of the car. At that moment, the bus arrived and Rocky leapt on, sitting down panting near the door, so that he could see what traffic was following. He was so concerned with this, he forgot about paying his fare until the conductor said,

"Come on, wack, where's yer money? Travelling free, are yer?"

Rocky pulled out a shilling.

"Pier 'ead."

And then he saw the Jag again, following behind. All right. It took them away from Joey, but what if Jim Simpson had decided to get rid of him also?

The streets were busy with early morning traffic, and the bus crawled down Church Street, stopping at every light and crossing, and so did the grey Jag. Sometimes it was so close that Rocky could make out Jim Simpson's malevolent eyes.

The bus reached Pier Head and Rocky leapt off, making for the landing stage and the snack bar. Inside it was hot, crowded and steamy. People stood and sat about with cups of coffee and bowls of soup. Outside, the mist had cleared from the river, and the waters of the Mersey were sullen and yellow. The New Brighton ferry boat stood with its gang-plank down. According to the clock, it was leaving in ten minutes.

Rocky looked round, pushing through the crowd, and then he saw Durr at his table in the corner, his bald head bent over a bowl of soup into which he was dropping pieces of bread, stirring the mixture round with a spoon, and looking at it with concentration.

Rocky was pushing towards him, when the door opened with a cold blast of air, and Jim Simpson and his body-guard shouldered their way in.

Rocky turned hastily towards the crowd at the counter. What was he to do? Maybe they wouldn't see him. But even if they did, they couldn't do much in this crowd. Best to act natural.

He counted over his money and ordered a cup of coffee. As the girl pushed it across the counter to him, Jim Simpson loomed at his side.

"Hello, there," he said.

"I'll have some sugar if yer don't mind," said Rocky to the girl, trying hard to keep his voice steady. Carrying his cup from the counter, he said to Simpson, "Get lost!"

He had a plan. If only it worked.

Casually he looked round for a seat. Only one empty—beside Durr.

"Mind if I ... "

Durr only looked up, bleary-eyed.

"Yer've got to listen to me, but don't say nothin' just now," said Rocky, desperately.

Durr blinked at him with red-rimmed eyes, and then returned to his soup, but Rocky felt he wasn't as stupid as he seemed.

"Joey sent me ... he wants to know if you can take him

away … on your boat … "

Durr wiped his mouth with his sleeve.

"It'll cost him something," he said under this cover.

"That's all right … what time?"

"I'll be leaving on the tide tonight … any time till then … "

Rocky looked round hastily. The two men were standing at the counter, watching him. He glanced through the window. They were just about to raise the gang-plank for the ferry to sail. "All right. He says he'll come tonight and yer to wait for him." Rocky leapt up, fought his way out of the snack bar and on to the landing stage. He rushed along shouting, and ran on to the gang-plank. The seaman shouted a warning, for the plank was already being raised, but Rocky leapt the short distance and landed on the deck.

"Yer know what's down there, don't yer, lad?" said a seaman, catching hold of him to steady him. "That's the Mersey down there, and it's deep!"

But Rocky, panting and breathless, was only interested in watching the distance widen between the boat and quay, and in seeing the frustration of Jim Simpson as he rushed to the water's edge, too late to get on the ferry.

CHAPTER
16

ROCKY had gone to the stern of the ship, up on the top deck, from where he could see Jim Simpson standing on the landing stage, his bulging eyes fixed angrily on Rocky. Then Simpson had turned and strode away.

The landing stage and the Liver Building retreated with the rest of Liverpool, as the ferry drew out into the river. A cloud of wheeling, white sea-birds followed in the wake of the ship, and a small boy standing with his mother at the rail threw pieces of bread to them. The birds swooped, catching the crumbs in mid-air, sending their raucous, lonely cries out into other noises of the river—the grind of the engine, the hooting of ships. It was grey cloud overhead, and grey river below, and a driving rain came down.

Rocky hunched into his anorak, and went down to the next deck which was covered. He shivered with cold. As the docks of Liverpool and Birkenhead slid by on each side, he could still see beyond the strangely shaped spire of the new Catholic cathedral, and beyond it the pink, oblong steeple of the Anglican cathedral that would still be looking down into the Square where Joey was hiding, and Mr Oliver cleaning out the old house, and his family at home all unaware of what was happening to him. Rocky had plenty of time to think things out on the ferry. If Jim Simpson was really out to get him, he would wait for him to get back to Liverpool, or he might drive his car through the tunnel and up to New Brighton and meet the ferry as it came in there.

Rocky decided his best plan was to dodge off the ferry carefully at New Brighton. Take the bus to Birkenhead and then the railway across to Liverpool. All this would take money. He investigated his resources in this field and found he would probably just have enough. Meanwhile, not having had much breakfast, he was getting hungry. Maybe he could just afford a Wagon Wheel from the buffet.

As the ferry came into New Brighton, he stood anxiously at the rail trying to catch sight of Jim Simpson, or of his grey Jag further on beyond the landing stage. So far as he could see, he wasn't there.

The green-roofed pavilions of New Brighton, the row of old houses facing the quay, the sea breaking white around the old fort—but so far, no sign of Jim Simpson's car.

Nevertheless, he kept in among the crowd as he left the boat and walked up the bridge to the turnstiles. Then there was a very dangerous, open walk to the bus stop, and the waiting there quite isolated.

Stamping his feet to keep warm, his thoughts concerned with Joey and his problems, it was not surprising that the grey Jaguar had moved silently alongside him before he realized it, and Jim Simpson was out and grabbing at him.

"Want a word with you ... "

He began dragging Rocky into the car but the process was rather like trying to push a blown-up balloon into a small box—whenever one part was pushed in, another part was sticking out. Rocky struggled, scratching and kicking and shouting.

But there was another man inside the car, pulling at Rocky, and Rocky hadn't a chance. In a few seconds he was inside, and the door had slammed, and the car was moving off.

Rocky struggled and fought in the back of the car like a wild animal, shouting whenever he could get his mouth from the man's hand.

"Shut him up, will yer!" shouted Jim Simpson.

"Shut him up! Yer should try it!"

"Shut him up!"

Rocky felt a sudden stunning thud on the back of his head, coloured stars shot about all around him, and then he was falling and falling, terrifyingly, into a deep, dark vacancy.

Dusk was falling when the wingy, who had worried all day about Rocky, set off across the Square towards number 3. He would call in on the Flanagans, just to see how things were. People didn't usually call in on each other in St Catherine's Square, though they would always pass the time of day when they met, but Mr Oliver hadn't seen Rocky about with the rest of the Cats that evening and he was worried.

He entered the hall and hesitated outside the living-room door. Then he heard Mr Flanagan's voice raised angrily, Mrs Flanagan screaming, and a thumping sound as though someone had fallen.

Mr Oliver knocked and pushed open the door.

Mr Flanagan was just picking himself up off the ground, and a young man was standing over him.

"I only want some cash," Joey was saying, in a quiet, sinister way that Rocky had never heard. "I'm not staying, see? I'm not coming back ter this! I want some cash and I'll clear out."

Mr Oliver put his pipe in his pocket.

"D'yer want any help here?" he asked.

"You keep out of this," said the young man.

"Yer'll get no cash from me," said Rocky's stepfather, sitting down, and dabbing a bleeding lip with his handkerchief. "I don't want to put yer back in the police hands, for yer mother's sake. But yer'll get no money, and yer'll get out now. Come back here, and I *will* get the police."

"No, no!" screamed Mrs Flanagan. "Yer can't tell the police! Here, Joey. I've got some money—here … "

She hunted up her purse, and thrust some notes at Joey.

"But, Joey, where yer going? Yer'll look after yerself, son?"

"Thanks, Mam. Don't worry. I'm all right. Terrah. Be seein' yer … "

Mr Oliver put his back against the door.

"Ye'd better get out of my way, mister."

"Is he to be let go?"

"Aye, let him go—and good riddance to him," said Mr Flanagan, and Joey pulled open the door and disappeared.

"I take it that was Joey. Are yer all right?" asked the wingy.

"I'm all right. This is a fine thing ter happen to a family."

"Joey never had a chance! He never had a chance," cried Mrs Flanagan.

"Never mind Joey. What about Rocky?" said the wingy. "I saw him this morning, and he looked worried."

"He's not back from school. Not been back all day, but I thought he was off on some game and would be in." Mr Flanagan began to put on his tie. "Maybe I'd better go down ter the police station and get them to keep a look out. With Joey going on like this, yer never know … "

"I'll walk down with yer, then … " said the wingy.

The first thing Rocky was aware of was voices—from a long way off.

"Yer sure yer haven't hit him too hard and put him away for good?"

"No—he's coming round now, look."

The blurred scene before Rocky's eyes sorted itself out. Half a dozen of Jimmy Simpson's face swam around and then merged into one.

"Aye. He's come round."

He was in a room—a strange room. Small, and with modern furniture, but cold, and unlived in.

"Rocky O'Rourke—are you hearing me all right?"

Rocky nodded.

"Where's yer brother Joey? Just tell me where he is, and yer can go home."

Rocky remembered everything very suddenly. He'd been kidnapped, and this was Joey's enemy. He couldn't tell them where Joey was. But if he didn't, they'd probably kill him. After all, he'd seen Jimmy Simpson on the *Rosemary*.

The electric light blazed into his face, hurting his eyes.

"What time is it? Is it night?"

"Yes, it's night."

"Me dad'll be after you. He'll have all the coppers out after you."

"Well, he'll not find us. Where's that brother of yours? Look, lad, tell us where he is, and you're free."

If it was night, then Joey would be gone. Away on Durr's boat. And if he did tell them where to look for Joey, maybe they'd leave him and he could escape.

"He's in the basement of the old vicarage in St Catherine's Square."

Jimmy Simpson's bulging eyes withdrew.

"Right," he said to the other man. "Let's get him."

"What about this one?"

"Lock him up. Bathroom's the safest bet. If his brother's

not where he says he is—we'll come back and finish him off. D'yer hear that, lad?"

The bathroom was small. There was one window above the lavatory—a small window. Rocky sat on the floor and looked at it. Then he stood on the lavatory and tried to open it. It opened easily enough, but there was a long drop to the ground, he thought, so far as he could make out in the darkness.

The damp breeze cleared his head a bit. He could hear sounds of the country—trees and grass rustling. Rocky got up on the window-sill and leant well out. There was a drain-pipe just at the side of the window. Well, it was worth a try. He edged out on to a narrow window-sill, one hand clutching the window-ledge, the other reaching out for the pipe. He grasped it, got one leg round it, and began to shin down. Once he almost lost his hold and fell. Thank the lord, he thought, for me Jesus-boots. At least they help yer to grip.

When he found himself on the ground among a heap of fallen leaves, Rocky suddenly felt dizzy. He vomited, and then leaned against the wall gasping. He seemed to be in some sort of garden. Unsteadily, he searched for a gate and found it. Ahead of him, across a field, were the flaring lights of a dual carriageway, the movement of traffic. Rocky stumbled towards it.

By the time he got there, his head had cleared and he recognized the road—it was the East Lancashire. It led straight into Liverpool. He would get a hitch.

It was eventually a lorry that pulled up beside him, and Rocky scrambled up into the cab.

"Where're yer heading for?" asked the driver.

"Liverpool."

"I can drop yer at Lime Street. All right? Late for a lad like you ter be out, isn't it?"

"I was out with me pals and got lost."

"Not running away, are yer?"

Rocky grinned, pallidly. "No, wack. I'm running back!"

Near Lime Street Station the lorry halted for a second to let Rocky out, and Rocky hurried along the pavement, busy with the late night crowds, to the station entrance. A cab was just pulling out into Lime Street.

"Hi, mister! Give's a lift!"

"Where yer heading?"

"Upper Parly."

"You're lucky. Get in."

Rocky got quickly into the back of the cab. It was warm and had a feeling of safeness about it.

"Just off to a call in Upper Parly. You're lucky," repeated the driver through the glass partition. "Lost yer bus fare?"

"Ay."

It was eleven o'clock when a dazed and sleepy Rocky fell through the door into the kitchen of number 3.

"Rocky!" Mr Flanagan rushed to help him up. "Are yer all right, lad? Where've yer been?"

"It was Jimmy Simpson. He kidnapped me. He wanted Joey, yer see … "

"Where's he now?"

"He'll be going back to the house—along the East Lancashire Road … "

"Look, Rocky, we'll have to go and get the police on ter this … "

"No—I'm tired. And I'm not scatting … "

"Rocky, till we get Simpson behind bars, yer'll not be safe—not after this. Come on, lad. Make the effort."

The rest of the events Rocky experienced through a haze of weariness. There were the explanations at the police station, sipping a cup of hot tea, the drive along the

131

East Lancashire Road in a police car, looking out for the house, and sure he wouldn't remember it until, "There it is!" And Jim Simpson's grey Jag outside again. They got both of them that night. But not Joey. Joey had got away.

CHAPTER
17

"Yer sure yer all right for going out?" asked Mr Flanagan.

It was late the next day, and Rocky, after a long sleep, was anxious to get out and tell his experiences to the Cats.

"Sure."

"Where'll yer be?"

"Just around ... "

"Well don't go far. We're going into town tomorrow—yer could do with some proper shoes, and some new clothes, and we're buying them straight off."

"All right! But I wouldn't have been without me Jesus-boots last night—coming down that drain-pipe ... "

The Cats were already gathered in a corner of the Square. They had heard many rumours, but they had to hear it from Rocky's own lips.

"Hi Rocky!"

"Hi Cats!"

"What happened ter yer, Rocky?"

"I was kidnapped. Jimmy Simpson got me. Mind, there was two to one, or they wouldn't have."

"Go on—yer codding! Jimmy Simpson was after your Joey," said the Nabber.

"I'll hang one on you Nabber Neville! I'm telling yer, I was kidnapped—you ask the scuffer!"

"It's my birthday tomorrow," said Billy, abruptly. "My mam says I can have a party and youse can all come."

"All the Cats?" Rocky, Beady, little Chan and the

Nabber looked unbelieving. They were not the kind who were usually invited to parties.

"She wasn't going to have youse, but now she says Rocky deserves it. Only we can't have a proper party because of the noise. We'll have tea and then she'll pay for us ter go ter the pictures."

"What about our Suzie? Can she come?"

"I expect so. I'm having a proper cake. It's in Millard's window down Upper Parly—they made it. It's got a chocolate car on top."

"Smashin'! See youse all termorrer then," said Rocky. "Hi, I'm goin' ter see the wingy. They're clearing all the furniture out of Mrs Aber's and they might have some things we can have for the hideout."

Mr Oliver was pleased to see him.

"Ah! Detective-Inspector O'Rourke, isn't it?" he grinned.

"Come off it, Mr Oliver. I'm no scuffer!" protested Rocky. "You know like, if there was any furniture yer didn't want, the gang'd like it."

"There might be one or two things. I'll keep it in mind. Oh, and Rocky—here, go and celebrate with that. I daresay yer'll know what to do with it … "

Rocky didn't have to think twice about that. He made his way straight to the Golden Salamandar, a misnamed snack bar of anything but a golden appearance off Upper Parliament Street. He went through the streets confidently, his hands thrust into his pockets. He whistled nonchalantly, and strode into the lighted cafe, straight up to the counter above which, unfortunately, his head only just showed.

Venturini, the owner, was a balding Italian. He looked down at Rocky.

"Yes?"

"A plate of chips, some bread 'n' butter, an' a cup of tea."

Venturini rased his eyebrows. Rocky shrugged and smacked the two shilling piece down on the counter. Then he swaggered to one of the tubular, plastic-topped tables beside the window. The table tops were red, the place was plastered with advertisements, lit with cold neon. Rocky's feet barely touched the floor when he sat down. But he was happy there. He liked the big red plastic bottle that you squeezed tomato sauce out of, and the big salt shakers. He liked to feel he was independent and important—and more than anything he liked the food. It was slid before you on a white bakelite plate—a pile of pale yellow chips, two rounds of bread and butter, a big cup of strong tea. Rocky sprinkled the chips liberally with salt, drowned them in a flowing tide of tomato sauce, and tucked in.

Erik Haugaard: *The Little Fishes*
Esther Hautzig: *The Endless Steppe*
Bessie Head: *When Rain Clouds Gather*
Ernest Hemingway: *The Old Man and the Sea*
John Hersey: *A Single Pebble*
Nigel Hinton: *Getting Free; Buddy*
Alfred Hitchcock: *Sinister Spies*
C. Walter Hodges: *The Overland Launch*
Richard Hough: *Razor Eyes*
Geoffrey Household: *Rogue Male; A Rough Shoot; Prisoner of the Indies; Escape into Dayl*
Fred Hoyle: *The Black Cloud*
Shirley Hughes: *Here Comes Charlie Moon*
Henry James: *Washington Square*
Josephine Kamm: *Young Mother; Out of Step; Where Do We Go From Here?; The Star Point*
Erich Kästner: *Emil and the Detectives; Lottie and Lisa*
M. E. Kerr: *Dinky Hocker Shoots Smack!; Gentlehands*
Clive King: *Me and My Million*
John Knowles: *A Separate Peace*
Marghanita Laski: *Little Boy Lost*
D. H. Lawrence: *Sea and Sardinia; The Fox* and *The Virgin and the Gypsy; Selected Tales*
Harper Lee: *To Kill a Mockingbird*
Laurie Lee: *As I Walked Out One Mid-Summer Morning*
Ursula Le Guin: *A Wizard of Earthsea; The Tombs of Atuan; The Farthest Shore; A Very F Way from Anywhere Else*
Doris Lessing: *The Grass is Singing*
C. Day Lewis: *The Otterbury Incident*
Lorna Lewis: *Leonardo the Inventor*
Martin Lindsay: *The Epic of Captain Scott*
David Line: *Run for Your Life; Mike and Me; Under Plum Lake*
Kathleen Lines: *The House of the Nightmare; The Haunted and the Haunters*
Joan Lingard: *Across the Barricades; Into Exile; The Clearance; The File on Fräulein Berg*
Penelope Lively: *The Ghost of Thomas Kempe*
Jack London: *The Call of the Wild; White Fang*
Carson McCullers: *The Member of the Wedding*
Lee McGiffen: *On the Trail to Sacramento*
Margaret Mahy: *The Haunting*
Wolf Mankowitz: *A Kid for Two Farthings*
Jan Mark: *Thunder and Lightnings; Under the Autumn Garden*
James Vance Marshall: *A River Ran Out of Eden; Walkabout; My Boy John that Went to A Walk to the Hills of the Dreamtime*
David Martin: *The Cabby's Daughter*
John Masefield: *The Bird of Dawning; The Midnight Folk*
W. Somerset Maugham: *The Kite and Other Stories*
Guy de Maupassant: *Prisoners of War and Other Stories*
Laurence Meynell: *Builder and Dreamer*
Yvonne Mitchell: *Cathy Away*
Honoré Morrow: *The Splendid Journey*
R. K. Narayan: *A Tiger for Malgudi*
Bill Naughton: *The Goalkeeper's Revenge; A Dog Called Nelson; My Pal Spadger*
E. Nesbit: *The Railway Children; The Story of the Treasure Seekers*
E. Neville: *It's Like this, Cat*
Mary Norton: *The Borrowers*
Robert C. O'Brien: *Mrs Frisby and the Rats of NIMH; Z for Zachariah*
Scott O'Dell: *Island of the Blue Dolphins*
George Orwell: *Animal Farm*
Katherine Paterson: *Jacob Have I Loved; Bridge to Terabithia*